The Game

Iryna Tsurek

The Game

Vanguard Press

VANGUARD PAPERBACK

A CIP catalogue record for this title is available from the British Library.

ISBN 978-1-83671-137-7

Vanguard Press is an imprint of
Pegasus Elliot Mackenzie Publishers Ltd.
www.pegasuspublishers.com

First Published in 2026

Vanguard Press
Sheraton House Castle Park
Cambridge England

Printed & Bound in Great Britain

Acknowledgment

I am sincerely grateful to everyone who has been with me and supported me on my creative journey.

First and foremost, to my parents: incredible people who sometimes seem ready to support any idea I have. Thank you for that!

Thanks to the team at my publishing house who carefully prepared the book for publication.

To my translator, Oleksandr Sorochan, we met by chance, but I'm so glad we became a team.

To my illustrator, Diana Kahlinska: although you won't see her artworks in the book, they already live on my page.

My team is made up of people, who help bring my ideas to life and give them breath.

Dedicated to all the girls who met the 'wrong' prince for the first time.

Playlist

🎧 "12 points" — for the whole book (by Jerry Heil)

She stayed silent for too long.
Now it's time to turn up the volume — even if the world isn't ready to listen.

💔 "Love Me Heart" — for all mentions of him (by Jerry Heil)

He says "love," but it sounds like a "game."
She smiles — because she knows the stakes are higher than they seem.

One of the most influential men in town desires her, knowing her only through gossip. The other is a skilled doctor who falls in love with the real her. Lilith faces a choice, a sea of intrigues, pain, disappointments, and emotional ups and downs—all in the pursuit of true love.

A white feather wished to write,
But lacked the skill to do it right.
Seeing another, craved to love,
Yet found just white paint's bluff.

Prologue

I remember the days when my dad got drunk and, as my brother later explained, threw things at Alex. It was always scary to watch. Once, when we came back from school, our father threw such a tantrum that Alex ended up in the hospital. His eyebrow was split—I saw that much, but I'm sure there was more. Because I was little, no one ever told me the full truth.

My brother and I are nine years apart, so when I was still very young, he took on all the responsibilities at home and with raising me. Since our father wasn't interested in us at all, it wasn't easy for my brother. I did what I could to help Alex, taking on cooking and cleaning duties myself.

Chapter 1

It's three a.m., and everyone in the dorm is asleep. I try not to think about the pain, jumping from one thought to another and fantasizing, but it doesn't work well. Every night, I have stomach pains. The doctor who examined me said they're hunger pains that arise from my condition. Many people online suggest always having some cookies or candy with you for such cases, but I don't think candy at night is a great idea. I left some cookies next to me twice, but when I woke up, they were gone—it's a dormitory after all, nothing strange. I tossed and turned in bed for another hour, and when I couldn't take it anymore, I crawled out from under the blanket, reached my closet, and got a glass of water. It temporarily eases the pain—I've checked.

"Lily, what's the matter? You woke me up in the middle of the night again. Are you thirsty again?" one of my neighbors asks.

"Yes, it's hot in here. That's probably why I'm so thirsty."

"You should probably go back to sleep before you wake the others. I don't want to see Olivia angry. She's terrible when she's angry, especially when she's disturbed from a pleasant sleep."

The water helped me sleep for another four hours. I was so comfortable that I didn't even want to think about breakfast. But I should have. At seven in the morning, one of my roommates' alarm clocks went off, and strangely enough, it woke everyone up except her. She only woke up after the three of us dragged her out of bed. Olivia loves to have a long, deep sleep, even though her phone can be heard by almost everyone on the floor.

We haven't known each other long, maybe two or three weeks since college started, but we've already learned each other's silly habits. One of Olivia's is that she likes to sleep for a long time. Emma is still afraid of monsters hiding under the bed, so every night she wraps herself up like a mummy, almost covering her head. She explains that leaving a limb uncovered is risky. Isabelle believes in ghosts and everything supernatural, so every night she turns the computer chair, toys, and mirrors away from her bed. She explains, "This is so that I'm not watched at night. Who knows who will want to sit on our chair if it's turned toward me? Even if that phantom doesn't want to look at me, it will have no choice."

I remember having great cooking skills since childhood. Since my mother died when I was little and my father passed away when I was in elementary school, the kitchen became my responsibility. I was pretty good at it, and according to my brother, I could have been a good chef—but somehow it didn't work out. At the last moment, I chose pedagogy and got into college without any problems.

After we finally managed to get Olivia out of bed, the battle for the bathroom began. We have one bathroom for four people, and there's really not enough time for everyone. In the morning, we remember our childhood, especially the game of tag, but the situation here is different from childhood. Back then, you ran after someone for fun, and it didn't matter if you were caught first or not. Now, you dream that everyone is chasing you, but you often aren't so lucky. Emma is always the fastest. She once told us the secret of her success: the monsters under her bed help her stay in great shape. She often runs from them at night—she trained.

"Girls, I'm first again today. The next one can go in twenty minutes. Good luck choosing your spots," Emma announced.

"I'm second."

"Third."

"And I'll be fourth." I exhaled heavily.

Emma had been in the shower too long, and with two other girls ahead of me, it was useless to expect even a couple of drops of warm water would be left. I didn't want to take any chances with the temperature drops, so I just brushed my teeth and ran out of the dorm. I had ten minutes to run two stops and get ready for class.

***

The classroom was buzzing with students waiting for the first class. Lily barely made it in time. She ran into the classroom and took her usual place at the back of the room, near a large cabinet with textbooks. She couldn't be called lonely or unattractive; she was pleasant and beautiful in her own way. Unlike the porcelain dolls her classmates resembled, Lily wasn't popular with the boys. Apparently, it's cool nowadays to be artificial, impudent, and feed your ego at every opportunity. Lily wasn't like that, and as a result, she became a black sheep among the popular girls. But she didn't care; she didn't seek common ground with people like them. Her roommates were enough for her to be friends with. Despite their different personalities, they all treated Lily as their equal, as it should be in a group of friends.

After her brother moved out, he left the house to Lily as a place she could live in and return to whenever she pleased. Yet, she clung to the last available place in the college dormitory with such desperation, as if her house was haunted. Perhaps, to her, it was. She remembered everything: the broken plates, cups, torn notebooks, and her dead father on the couch, gone for years now. Her eyes recalled every detail vividly, and it frightened her. She couldn't bring herself to fall asleep in that house—too many thoughts, memories, and emotions, and a sense of fear.

Lily did really well in her studies, which totally annoyed the girls who thought they were the elite of the group. She couldn't care less about their dirty looks and attempts to embarrass her. If this had happened two years ago, her confidence would've taken a nosedive. But now, things were different. She wouldn't cry over being publicly humiliated anymore; instead, she might cry her heart out at home. She still didn't trust people and kept making the same mistakes with some of them. That's life—unpredictable. Even if someone had warned her about the troubles she'd face in college today, how would that change things? What could she do differently armed with that knowledge?

In the girls' group, students were mostly divided into two types: those who enjoyed nighttime walks with friends, cigarettes, or the trendy 'e-cigs' and 'vapes,' along with alcohol, cocktails, and wine—often smelled even during class from an innocent-looking 'Fresh Juice' box in someone's hand. Then there were those contents to relax in bed with a cup of tea or coffee and a good book. Each would likely become different kinds of teachers in the future, finding their own ways to connect with children and make life easier. Sure, a few stood out due to their parents' wealth and savings, but every group probably has someone like that.

Lily belonged to the second group. She was among the few who didn't enjoy noisy gatherings, nighttime darkness, or the smell of cigarette smoke.

Chapter 2

I've overcome my fear of my peers. It wasn't easy, and it took a while, but now I couldn't care less about their words. Let them have their fun. However, the fear of older people, especially men, has been etched into my memory since childhood. Now, I sit at the front desk at the teacher's request—a man in his fifties who thinks all my good grades are just luck or that I was cheating on the back desk. So, after everyone finished the test that he probably spent days crafting, he started questioning me and a few other students whose grades he doubted. He drilled us on everything we covered in the previous class. By question eight, he began to panic as he veered off-topic, eventually circling back to the introductory lecture. I didn't cram; I've just learned what I need to know in life, and after successfully avoiding a well-planned public humiliation, I'd say the day started perfectly.

***

"Okay, Lilith, you've proven that you listen to me sometimes, but I think most of those questions were too easy for your level"—he glanced around at the group—"so you're just lucky," the man said, discreetly wiping sweat from his face.

"If you have any more questions, we can continue." Lily smiled sincerely at him, looking expectantly.

"No, girl, we won't continue," he replied sternly. "But I'd like you to sit right at the front desk in my classes so I can keep an eye on you, so no one passes love notes or distracts you during tests."

"Oh, come on, who's going to write her those notes? Maybe she's going to write them to herself in advance?" a voice from the back teased.

The remark amused the class, but the teacher tried to keep his face emotionless, choosing not to address the interruption.

"I hope you understand, Miss Lilith," he concluded.

"Yes, I do," she replied calmly.

Till the end of the day, Lily was sitting at the last desk, but the next day she moved to the front row. Every time she took her seat there, she overheard comments like:

"Holy shit, seriously?"

"Why in front of me? What did I do?"

"He really doesn't like her, that's good, unlike other teachers who are too nice and give her good grades for a few words."

The next morning, she snagged second place in the shower line, so she had to arrive early for class. Then the weekend came. Although she could have gone home, the thought of that place scared her. She had lived alone in that house for too long to want to return. While she really loved her brother, she didn't love that place. Perhaps Alex could find time to go for a walk with her, and it would be nice if he could bring Dylan along.

I think spending the day out with Alex, and then returning to the dorm in the evening, would be the best plan.

She quickly typed a message to her brother:

"Hey Alex, are you busy this weekend? If not, I'd love to go out with you guys. It would be great. I promise not to bother you much." She giggled as she typed, putting on her best face. "I'm off to class now. Waiting for your reply! XOXO"

The reply came promptly. "Hi, Lily, no problem. Just let me know when to pick you up. Have a great day!"

"You too."

***

The walk was like a boost of energy for the next week, with a warm and pleasant atmosphere, and bright emotions—everything that Lily would like to feel every day. First, they went to a restaurant and had a delicious lunch with potatoes, which Lily loved, and two types of salads that were also among her top preferences. They then decided to take a walk in the park. The girl's phone gallery was filled with photos of the three or two of them together, but rarely alone; she didn't like to take pictures of herself. They weren't the right emotions. The photos with Alex and Dylan radiated sincere joy. How could you capture that alone?

The trio ended the day at the movies, facing a choice between drama, thriller, and mystery. Their opinions split dramatically, so they settled on something neutral—a comedy. The cinema was packed, making it challenging to find three seats together. Eventually, Dylan bought three tickets: two together and one over one seat from them. Five minutes later, he returned with a new ticket next to the seat next to theirs, evidently having swapped seats with the person between them. The comedy was light, and the plot was interesting, akin to a fairy tale.

At the end of the day, the guys gave Lily a lift to the dorm. At its entrance, there were enough girls who only waited for a chance to gossip. Among their chitchat, Lily distinctively heard:

"Have you seen the way she's dressed? 'Oh, I'm an innocent orphan, I have no money,' and look at her now."

"Who cares about her clothes? Did you see what car she got out of?"

"Yeah, I did. I was wondering if she works as a housemaid in the owner's house. Maybe they felt sorry for her and ordered someone to drive Lilith to the dorm. Or was it out of gratitude? What do you think? Isn't it fitting that her name coincides with the night deviless?"

"You've got quite the imagination. Who would hire her? She's just a plain orphan Jane. Who knows what to expect from them," said the girl standing to Lily's left, prompting laughter from the crowd. Someone chimed in that she looked more like a deviless, blending their words with the laughter around them.

"I see you're having a good time; I won't spoil it."

But why am I suddenly being called a deviless? I'm curious to know. I can't pretend to get along with everyone or wear a constant smile on my face—I reserve that for genuine happiness and meaningful relationships. Why waste my energy on those who don't need it anyway? This isn't about teachers or adults; it's about my classmates who act like royalty, expecting everyone to bow to them. If they're fine with that, let them have it. But as for me, why should I? Am I supposed to be their Cinderella? No thanks. I have a good life with Emma, Olivia, and Isabel. It's a shame they're not in my class.

***

Lily spent that night and the next day alone, curled up in her bed, scrolling through her Instagram feed, looking for something interesting, but it was full of students partying. Her friends were always dispersed to their friends' and parents' on weekends, so Lily had plenty of time to read.

She loved novels, especially fantasy—worlds of fairies, mermaids, and elves—a fascination not many people knew she had. Books calmed her down, motivated her, and gave her strength. She viewed different situations from both the author's and an imaginary character's perspectives. Sometimes, it was morally challenging, but not as tough as for the character described by the book's author. Such moments reminded her to appreciate the little things, and she realized that many of the problems we often discuss with friends and family, considering them the end of the world, aren't really so.

Chapter 3

"I've got some amazing news for you girls; listen to what I'm about to tell you," Emma said, holding her breath as she looked at her friends. "You know Dan, the senior? He's having a party at his house, and I'm invited. When I asked if I could bring some friends, he said, 'Yeah, sure, the more people, the better, right?'" Emma was jumping up and down as she spoke. "Any complaints, suggestions, or wishes?"

"Yes, I have one. You've come out of the blue with this proposal, and I don't even know what to say," said Isabelle.

"I don't mind," Olivia said lazily.

"I'm afraid it's not my kind of company, and I'm not sure I'd feel comfortable there, so I'll probably pass."

"Come on, Lily, you only live once, and these opportunities don't come around often," Emma replied, pushing her toward the mirror. "Have you thought about what you're going to wear or what kind of makeup you'll have?"

"No, I haven't. Does it even matter? I'm not going for a show, and I don't plan to meet anyone there." Lily shrugged.

"No, no, no, darling, you're wrong. A girl should always be perfect, perfectly dressed, neat, and with a pleasant smell of perfume."

"Isn't the soul more important? Yes, I agree, the first impression is significant, but clothes and makeup are just images, and everyone has a different taste in images."

"Dear, I understand what you're saying. Still, the world is cruel, and few people pay attention to intelligence, sincerity, and all that stuff we want to treasure in ourselves. Okay, it looks like I need to take care of things myself. Isabelle, hand me the hair straightener. We have some work to do."

***

Thirty minutes later, I was standing in a nice dress with matching heels, holding the handbag Emma had lent me for the evening, sparkles over my eyes, and my hair falling like silk on my shoulders.

We took a taxi to that senior guy's house. He lives in an elite area of the city, and it's not surprising—you could tell just by the way people talked about him. I don't know whose son, brother, or whatever he is, but he definitely has some money. They say he lives alone in this massive house. It wouldn't surprise me if I heard that cleaners and gardeners work here around the clock—the property is just insanely huge.

When we entered the gate, I couldn't see where the garden ended, and the edges of the fence were hidden among the trees. After about six minutes of walking through the labyrinth of hedges and garden paths, we finally saw the house. It was large, two—maybe even three stories tall. In the twilight, it was hard to tell.

We were led to the hall where guests had already gathered. There was no dress code, so everyone wore what they were comfortable in, but it was easy to spot the expensive clothes. Exquisite dresses hugged the girls' waists, emphasizing all their curves, while the guys mostly wore shirts and dark slacks that looked like regular clothes but screamed money from a distance. We went to the table and grabbed a drink each. Emma said it looked like a typical posh evening for the rich now, but later things would heat up. The girls agreed, even though it was their first time there. They had heard plenty from Emma about the previous party that week.

Looks like just another excuse to blow their parents' money and show off, I thought.

From the beginning, everyone split into groups and chatted about everything, occasionally sipping their drinks. The regulars looked with interest at the 'fresh meat' that seemed out of place. Then we heard a door open somewhere on the second floor, and the owner of the house and his friends came down the stairs.

"Hello, good to see you all. It's great that you could find the time to come to my house tonight. I know this is the moment you've all been waiting for, so I'm happy to announce the start of the party," Dan said.

Everyone clapped as he turned off the lights in the room and started to walk down the stairs. A moment later, one of the guys behind him turned on the music and another switched on the lights, which flashed to the rhythm of the music.

Emma immediately dragged Isabel and Olivia to dance, and they pulled me in as well. We danced in the center of the room among hot, sweaty bodies. I can't say that dancing isn't my thing, but it's uncomfortable, especially when you turn your head and see dozens of guys standing against the wall, watching the dancers with great interest. Gross. I drank half a glass of some cocktail and immediately regretted it. A burning, acute pain like a dagger in my stomach prevented me from straightening up, but I stayed on my feet.

***

"Hey, Matt, have you chosen a date for tonight?" Jean asked.

"Surprisingly, not yet, but I'm hesitating between that girl by the speaker in the red dress and the shy one in the center of the dance floor."

"You have a strange taste, always hesitating," Jean said, clapping him on the shoulder.

"And you, my friend, never hesitate, and that's your mistake," Matt replied.

"So, guys, I propose we add some pleasant and joyful notes to our party. I'm ready to bet a hundred that I can conquer any girl you choose today," Dan said with a confident smile.

"A hundred for two?" Matt turned and asked Jean.

"I can do it. I already have an option."

"All right, let's go check if our options match."

"Guys, I see you're having fun already," Dan said, a sly smile stretching across his face.

"Yes, and believe me, it's only going to get more fun. Get your money ready. Today we'll make money on your fiasco."

Less than two minutes later, the two guys approached Dan again, exchanging a mysterious look. He looked up from his phone and asked, "Well, is everything set?"

"We've set in a decision. Your task is to ask out that girl in the center of the hall who acts like a robot after catching our eyes," the guys said, glancing at Lily.

She shuddered again.

"Are you kidding? That's too easy. I know her type—they immediately grab the best option, and in this case, it's me. You sure you won't regret losing your money so easily?"

"We'll see."

"Good luck; you'll need it."

He rolled his eyes, picked up two glasses of red wine, and moved into the crowd. *These idiots really think I'm a nobody here? Is there a girl who will turn me down? Funny. I've never met one in my twenty years. Usually, girls cling to me like leeches, impossible to shake off. Some even hunted for me after rejection, tracking down my phone number and address. Only God knows how they managed that because I always told my friends to keep quiet. Up close, she's a simple girl. No matter how she's dressed or what makeup she has on, her true self can't be hidden.*

"Hi, gorgeous, do you have a minute?"

Lily didn't realize he was talking to her at first. "Hi, did you want something?"

"I've been watching you. You're so pretty and elegant. I wanted to get to know you." Dan's smug expression never left his face.

"I see," the girl answered and turned to her friends.

For a moment, Dan was frozen but then put his hand on her shoulder. "You haven't answered yet; do you mind getting acquainted?"

"With whom?"

"With me, of course." He smiled.

"I do mind," Lily said without thinking for a second.

"Wait, what? Why?"

"I'm not interested."

"You're kidding. You don't get an offer like this every day, and you'll regret it."

"Are you a new laptop at a discount or something? Trust me, I'll get over it somehow."

"You're strange. Why pass up a chance that fate gives you?"

"Fate, you say?" She examined him with her eyes. "I take everything I can from fate, but I need nothing from you, thanks. Let those girls over there, who are drooling over you, take the chance."

"You sure?"

"Yeah, I don't see the point in repeating myself. Or do you have something substantial to interest me?"

"You could have said so right away." He swept his hair back and smiled. "Money or something more tangible; what exactly do you want?"

"I want to be sure of my guesses about you, but I can see everything here with the naked eye," she said, crossing her arms over her chest.

"What do you see then?"

"A rich daddy's boy who was born with a golden spoon in his mouth and thinks that everyone should polish it, pick it up from the floor if necessary, and bring it to him. But what a bummer, I won't fall for your charms. Sorry, you're not my type. I'll probably go now, lost my mood," Lily said as she headed to the wardrobe, picked up her purse, or rather her friend's purse, and stepped outside.

Dan stood in a daze for a long time, as if after a slap. He saw his friends waving to him like 'Come to us, tell us how it went,' but instead, he ran out into the street, gasping for air. But Lily had already left.

Chapter 4

I was walking through the dark streets, pressing my stomach against my spine with all my might—it hurt, it hurt a lot. And that guy, what was his name again? Dan. Damn him! Thought he could play a joke? He picked the wrong girl!

I was glad there were lots of cars driving by, and one of them stopped for me. It gave me a lift almost to the dorm, and then I walked the rest of the way. Water wouldn't help my stomach, I knew that, but I had no medicine on hand. The painkillers didn't help, and the medication the doctor had prescribed earlier had long since stopped working. So, I went to the bathroom, took a shower, prepared things for tomorrow, drank two cups of cool water, and went to bed. I tried to fall asleep until the pain subsided slightly.

The next day, I heard new rumors about me—something about being a mouse from a village yard who dared to turn her nose up when Dan tried to approach me, and more about how I dared to refuse him at all. It was mostly the girls gossiping. The guys, on the other hand, were divided into two groups: those who considered me gray and unworthy of attention and those who laughed at Dan's fiasco. Personally, I didn't care about either group. It was their opinion, and I respected it, but it wouldn't affect my behavior.

After the first class, my friends ran into my classroom, out of breath. I could tell from their faces that they had a lot of questions for me. Given that Emma came running in without her phone to be seen anywhere—a thing she never let out of her hand—I realized how serious this was for them.

"What did you do at Dan's party last night?"

"And why do we have to hear about it from gossip all over the college?"

"I don't think it was anything serious. Am I the only one who doesn't understand why everyone is making such a big deal out of it?"

"Yes, you're the only one who doesn't get it, darling. You really don't understand what you've done? You 'slapped' the college prince yesterday—he's probably never experienced such a thing before, and in his own house. Don't you think that's a disaster?"

"No, but are you suggesting I should have conversed with a guy I find unpleasant?"

"No, but—"

"You see, I did the right thing."

"You're weird."

"Really weird."

"I agree, I am weird. I wonder why I like this title? Perhaps because it distinguishes me from the crowd of his fans?"

***

Today, the team my brother coaches is playing against last year's champions. Dylan asked me to come and support him, and I was planning to go anyway. Alex has become a great coach in recent years. He doesn't make much money, but he doesn't need more than he has, considering he doesn't pay rent.

My brother still keeps in touch with his former team. I remember watching their games with fascination; they were like untouchable stars to me. At such games, Alex often has Gary, Dylan, Jason, and those who can take a break from hard work to enjoy the game. The first reaction from the guys on the 'Panthers,' who are coached by my brother, is always priceless—it's like meeting your favorite author at school and finding out she's your new literature teacher. Now, they're just proud they can ask for advice from former champions, two-time champions at that.

I love my brother, really, and I like this noisy company. I guess I'm just used to it. Many times, former members of the Panthers team gathered in our old house. It's amazing how they all fit in there. Those evenings felt like being part of a large, friendly family. I became an older sister to Jason and Alice's daughter, and they were like parents to me.

After school, I went to Alex's work, and from there we all went to the game at the opponents' school. All of my brother's students are almost my age, some a little older. I see them often, so they are as used to me as they are to each other, and I feel comfortable with them. I love volleyball. I tried to play since I was a kid, but it didn't quite work out. I probably don't have as much passion for it as Alex, who is ready to give it all his free time.

I was brought up by the 'Panthers,' so it's not surprising that I have the most pleasant and warmest memories associated with them. The game ended with our victory. It's an incredible feeling to see the stands packed with people cheering for your team. The hall exploded with emotion. The guys almost threw me and my brother on the floor with joy. I understand them—I often saw such emotions in my brother. When you train long and hard and finally achieve what you've been working toward, you're filled with relief and euphoria.

In the evening, I returned home, took a shower, had dinner, and fell asleep. In the morning, I remembered that my undone homework was still in my bag...

Chapter 5

"Hi, girl, you're up late today," Olivia said smiling.

"Yes, I overslept, and I don't even want to bring it up, because my next question is: 'Why didn't you wake me up?'"

"Strange, because we tried, right, girls?"

"Yeah, but you were so sound asleep."

"I understand, the dream must have been very interesting. I'm glad that at least I'm not late for class."

"Oh yeah, about class, someone is waiting for you in your classroom."

"Who?"

"You'll see. We've done our part and we're off to our classes."

"Intriguing…"

Lily walked a couple of steps down the corridor and opened the door to the classroom with a squeak. The first thing that caught her eye was a bunch of students, mostly girls, giggling and not taking their eyes off the center of the circle. It was impossible to see who was in the center; they had all the gaps tightly plugged. When Lily approached, they all quieted down, and the figure in the center seemed to appreciate the reaction of the girls he had been flirting with a few seconds ago and jumped to his feet.

"Howdy. I've been waiting for you," Dan said.

"I noticed," Lilith answered, glancing around the circle of girls.

"We were just discussing the next class, nothing important," he mumbled, stepping out of the circle. "Here, take these. They're beautiful, aren't they?"

"Yes, they are, but I'm sorry, I'm not so cruel as to keep them on my desk for another seven hours in this heat. I think you'll find a better use for them."

"Then why are you being so cruel to me?" He showed his signature predatory smile again.

"And how should I react to flowers from a guy to whom I clearly explained that I'm not interested in him as a man?"

If there had been whispers from the circle behind these words, now there was dead silence. Everyone turned their shocked eyes to Lilith, looking at her as if for the last time.

"I see, you must be joking, beauty. When did that happen?"

"At your party, sunshine. Have you forgotten?"

"Weird, I don't remember. Maybe you're confusing me with someone else?"

"Weird, indeed. Your frightened face was hard to confuse with another. Oh yeah, maybe we should ask the guys who were with you about this situation. They should be in the class next door."

"We'll be right back," Dan said to the others, grabbing Lilith's arm with a deadly grip and pulling her into the corridor. His grip loosened when he heard the door close. "What the hell are you doing?"

"Shouldn't I be asking you that? I just want to be left alone and not have you in my sight. Okay, I'm going to ask you, what the hell are *you* doing? It seems absurd for the college prince to seek attention from an ordinary girl."

Dan laughed but quickly calmed himself down. "Sorry, you're right. You're ordinary, but even an ordinary girl can interest a prince. Are you satisfied with my answer?"

"No. Now do me a favor: get lost."

"Sure, I was doing exactly that in your classroom."

"Having fun?"

"Yep."

"Good for you."

Lily walked past Dan back into the class, taking advantage of his dumbfoundedness. The door squeaked open, and all eyes were on her as she walked to her seat with an emotionless expression.

"No wonder there's an expression: 'Like a ghost passed by,'" said one of the girls watching.

"I agree. I got goosebumps on my arms when she came in!"

"It wouldn't have happened if you had dressed for the weather."

***

At the end of the first class, Lily received a message from her friends on her phone:

"We are waiting for you in the cafeteria at the table by the window. We need to talk!"

"I think I understand what it's about, but in any case, there are still forty minutes until the next class. I think there's enough time to discuss everything."

Two minutes later, Lily went down to the cafeteria, which was packed with hungry students, making the morning trolley seem quite comfy in comparison. It took her a while to get to the tables, but she quickly found her friends there.

"Sit down, we need to talk," said Isabelle.

"Here, have a drink. And help yourself with a sandwich," Emma added.

"Thanks, what do you want to talk about?"

"Eat first."

"Okay." Lily chewed slowly, the obviously not fresh bits of ham were peeking out from between the dark lettuce as the girls kept looking at her. "Say it already! I can't eat with people looking at me like that."

"Okay, we want to hear about Dan coming to see you today."

"I see, and?"

"And? What do you mean? Lilith, honey, every other girl in and out of our college wants to be with this guy. And you will just pass such a chance?"

"Girls, what chance are you talking about? Tell me you're joking. It's not funny. You're praising him like he's a saint."

"Within our school, yes!"

"Okay, I hear you. So, what should we talk about next?"

"We don't want situations like this one to repeat. We're worried about you, can't you see? He has his own fan club, and the girls in it are ready to do anything to any girl who shows him attention or tarnishes his reputation. But if you're together, you'll be under his protection. Do you understand?" Emma said.

"No, I don't understand, and I don't want to go into the details of this 'caste system.' Girls, can't you understand me? I don't like him at all…"

"Yes, dear, we can imagine how you feel, and believe us, you will be really happy with him," said Olivia, who for a moment seemed lost in her dreams.

"Do you really think so?"

"Sure. A year ago, he was dating a girl who had just graduated from college. He took her out to restaurants, picked her up from college and took her home, gave her expensive gifts, and I suspect that's not all."

"I don't know if there's any happiness in his money, and it's not even his…"

"Well, you need to try at least. In any case, you can always just break up."

"To be honest, I don't like your idea at all."

"You will thank us later."

"We'll see," she said as she walked to the classroom.

***

The idea was really stupid as if they were trying to give me away to the first best guy. Ridiculous! My stomach told me that my guesses about the freshness of the ham in the sandwich were right, so I had to wash the pain down with water again and promise myself never to eat in the cafeteria again.

Before I went to the dorm, I quickly replaced the books in my locker with the ones I would need tomorrow and went to the restroom, which was empty and quiet. I took advantage of the moment, quickly combed my hair, and put on some lipstick. A pretty girl was looking at me in the mirror. Confident, beautiful, with a look that was ready to withstand any difficulties. I ran my hand over the outline of the face I saw in the mirror. She didn't look plain and boring at all.

Smiling to myself, I picked up my things and pulled the door handle, but it didn't move. I tried a few more times, and then again, until panic took over. My palms were sweating, and I could feel my heart pounding as I fumbled for my phone. Outside, the sky was getting darker because of the clouds, and there were probably only a few people left in the college, given the high probability of a rainstorm.

In a panic, I started dialing my friends' numbers one by one. Emma was out of reach, and Olivia wasn't picking up. I tried to call Isabel, and as soon as she picked up, my phone went black. Shit! I stood there clutching it for a minute, wondering what to do. My brother doesn't come here—there's no point for him to commute for so long for some stupid thing.

I pulled myself together and looked around the bathroom, at the big heavy door, the air vent, and the one small window under the ceiling, which, no matter how hard I tried, I could only get my arm through. So, the only sensible solution that came to my mind was to knock on the door. Sooner or later, someone would definitely hear me.

I thought so until it was completely dark outside. Someone might say, "What's the problem? Just switch on the light, and that's it, magic, you're not in the dark." And I would just smile sincerely at such a genius as if I didn't think about it without his help. But I'll tell you what I'm gonna ask the audience: "Is there anyone who has learned to walk through walls in this world, for fuck's sake? At least partially?" *I just need to turn on the light, my ass.* The switch is in the hallway!

Luckily, in about two hours, according to my calculations, a security guard was walking around the college. He was my savior. The man was quite surprised to see me there, but I didn't want to give any explanations. And what could I say? Someone was bored and it was a prank? We both went out into the hall, and when he was closing the door again, I saw a small piece of paper that was somehow stuck to the wall near the door.

"There is a price for everything, there is a reckoning, and the punishment doesn't always come after you have tasted the forbidden fruit. It is often introduced in advance, so that no one comes close to what is divine and untouchable."

I decided not to tell anyone about this situation.

***

The next day, Dan was waiting for me in my class again, and after another day, I started to get used to it. What else could I do? I couldn't force him out of here, and it seemed like he didn't understand human speech. Every day, I caught the girls' sideways glances at me when Dan left a bunch of roses on my desk again. I don't like these flowers—they are red as if dipped in blood and prickly, their thorns like in that fairy tale about Sleeping Beauty, where you prick yourself and fall asleep forever. That's what I expected from Dan. And the flowers reminded me of myself: I'm not going to let strangers come to me easily either, and it's not going to be easy with me.

Dan came every day for a week, and every day I tried my best to ignore him—even when other gifts were added to the flowers. The girls fussed and the boys openly laughed at Dan chasing a simpleton, even though he was chased by a horde of models.

After the day I promised myself not to eat in the college cafeteria anymore, we went to eat in the cafe across the street. The food was not much better, but at least it was fresh. There were moments when I thought I saw Dan at the cash register or a few tables away, but when I looked in that direction again, he was gone.

"Hello, beauties, can I sit next to you?"

I did see him after all...

"Of course, sit down, sit down," Emma said, moving over to make room for him right in front of me.

"It's cozy in here," Dan said thoughtfully.

"It *was* cozy," I said through clenched teeth.

"I agree, it is not like the college cafeteria."

"Yeah, we come here a lot, if you want to come with us," Isabelle suggested playfully, apparently not having seen my murderous look or just pretending not to notice.

"Thank you, I will definitely take you up on your offer. That's why I came to you, Lilith. I have a question of life and death for you." He was quiet and caught my gaze. His eyes were dark and deep; they beckoned to me one moment, and the next, they frightened me with their depth.

Making sure he had my full attention, he continued, "Do you mind being my girlfriend?" He had a playful smile on his lips.

Emma dropped her fork, and Isabel choked on her water—or was it Olivia? My stone face twitched an eyebrow for a second, and that was it. The hall was quiet. Those who were nearby waited for my answer, and those who were sitting in the distance tried to understand what was happening.

"Thank you, but no," I answered.

Now Dan's eyebrow twitched. "Let me give you some time to think."

"Nothing will change."

"Lily, you really need to take some time. We're sure you'll change your mind," Emma said, trying to put out the fire that Dan's and my eyes had started.

"Oh great, I'll see you after school. I'll be waiting for an answer. Girls, do you need a ride home?"

"I said—"

"That would be great, I'll see you later," Emma replied with a big smile, one hand clasping mine.

"You're joking."

"No, dear, we're making a good life for you."

***

I had a long conversation with my friends about how I had no idea how well I would live in a relationship with him or how my popularity would grow in the college, about how I had failed to see such possibilities myself, and much more. And when I said that I had seen everything clearly, they gave me an ultimatum: either I start dating him, or we are no longer friends, and I am kicked out of the room. They would do it with three votes against one. This is insane!

I listened for a long time about all my future prospects and what I may lose if I refuse. I liked the phrase I heard them say, "Try it for a start; no one will force you to date him for a long time." I tried to imagine what my brother would do in my place. He would probably agree but would be on the lookout even in the safest and calmest situations. He would not trust anyone, and neither would I. It's just a game; maybe it's really worth a try?

I spent the day thinking about whether I should start this damn game, play a happy couple in public, and whether I should play at all. Doubts tormented me until I left the college, where he, with his huge smile, was waiting for us… For me.

"Hop in, I'll give you a ride," he said as he opened the back door of the car. The girls got in one by one, and when I wanted to sit down next to them, he blocked the way and opened the front door. "You're coming this way, do you mind?" I didn't answer; I just nodded, and his smile grew even wider.

"She has something to say to you, don't you, Lilith?"

"Yeah, I do, but I could have done it myself." I furrowed my brows. *Why do they need to hurry me up?* "Dan, I don't mind."

"Don't mind what, darling?"

"Don't mock me; you know what I mean."

"Maybe I do; maybe I don't. I can't read your mind yet, but I'll try to learn. So will you tell me what you don't mind?" He tried his best to hide the smile that was growing with each passing second. Others wouldn't have noticed, but I did.

"I'm not against the relationship," I voiced.

"Really? So, you've thought it over?" he asked with the same expression.

"Yes."

"Then that's great. So tomorrow we have our first date. Where would you like to go, beauty?"

"I'm sorry, what?" I asked in confusion.

"What's wrong? We've officially just become a couple, so where should we go? Or should I choose for the first time?"

"Do whatever you want."

He couldn't hide his broad smile any longer, and I had no desire to turn to the back seat.

Dan drove us to the dormitory. The girls thanked him and jumped out of the car, but when I wanted to get out, I felt strong resistance. He held my hand and looked directly into my eyes; his smile was still shining on his face.

"Give me your number."

"Can't we exchange numbers tomorrow, on our date?"

"We can, sure, but what should I do if I want to wish you sweet dreams before going to bed?"

"I don't know; maybe go to bed and think about a wonderful tomorrow?"

"I agree, tomorrow will be a wonderful day. But you know, I think I've found a solution. I'll come by in the evening, wish you sweet dreams, admire you…"

I froze for a moment at this thought and hesitated. "No, I don't think one message at night will hurt. I'm afraid if I see you here at night, I'll get sunburned by your crown. Write down the number."

"That's better. Read it clearly."

When I told Alex about today's situation, I heard nothing good except that I made the right decision as if Dan shouldn't be walking under my windows at night. Maybe I don't know my brother well enough to think that he would have done the same, or maybe he just doesn't want guys around me. Like, I can't have guys around me but he can? Not fair.

Chapter 6

After classes, Dan was waiting for me in his car at the main entrance. It was black, beautiful, and looked insanely expensive. I could see the girls looking at Dan and the guys looking at his car, then I saw a lot of stares at me. I hurried to the car, quickly opened the back door on the opposite side of Dan, and got in.

"Not there; please sit next to me, or do you want to have a date in the car? By the way, I've never tried it," he said. "Sounds interesting."

"No, thanks," Lilith replied, slamming the back door and sitting beside Dan.

"That's better."

"I'm glad. So where are we going?"

"First, we'll go shopping to update our wardrobe."

"And then what?"

"We're not done shopping yet, don't get ahead of yourself, darling."

I rolled my eyes and said nothing, and Dan was only amused.

The shopping trip was quite exhausting. I'm not used to spending several hours in a fitting room trying on exquisite, expensive clothes. A few hours that would have been a pleasure for a normal girl gave me only burning hunger. Under normal circumstances, I would have curled up and waited until the pain went away, but in front of Dan, I wasn't going to do that. It was hard to keep a stony face and smile at him from time to time, with sweat dripping down my forehead, but that wasn't the last drop of patience I had for the pain.

Dan chose a white shirt. I didn't see what brand it was, but the seller was thrilled to see someone buying it. I chose a sky-blue dress, not without Dan's help. He said that this dress was created to match my golden curls and blue eyes. And I, in turn, noted that his brown trousers looked harmonious with his brown eyes.

Dan took us to the most expensive restaurant in the city. They say that only millionaires, politicians, businessmen, or people like that eat there—in other words, the city's elite. As we were led to the hall, I was afraid my new shoes might accidentally damage the floor. Everything in the hall looked like it was made of gold. Gold alternated with gilding, and the floor was no exception.

We were led to a table by the window that overlooked the city center. While I was lost in my thoughts, we were handed the menu, and I was really scared to look at it. I couldn't even imagine how many zeros there were for the cheapest dish. And I was right, the menu listed only simple drinks, yet they cost as much as my stipend for half a year—too exquisite and too expensive.

"Haven't made up your mind yet?" Dan smiled.

"No, it's my first time here, so I don't even know what I'll like. Can I ask you to choose for me?"

"Sure."

He didn't hesitate for a moment before making his choice. He just said two words to the waiter, "As usual," and then turned his attention back to me. He was smiling, and I was fidgeting uncomfortably in my chair. When our food arrived, the first problem I faced was choosing the right fork. I know it sounds ridiculous, but there were a lot of them.

Dan must have seen the panic in my eyes and said, "Don't worry, use any you want. There aren't many people here; no one will notice."

How nice of him to say that instead of helping me. I could have asked him for help and made myself look even more ridiculous than I already did in his eyes, but that was the last thing I wanted to do. My stomach was churning, and it was begging for food. So, I just decided to choose the most comfortable fork and threw a piece of fish into my mouth. Dan watched me the whole time, then he took a completely different fork and started eating too. I knew what he was waiting for—my mistake. But I wasn't going to let it bring me down or change my fork just to please him because the fish tasted so delicious.

"Do you like it?" he asked with a predatory smile.

"Yes, I do."

"I'm glad; I'm really glad. So, where do you want to go next?" he asked, staring straight at me as I chewed and prayed that the piece wouldn't get stuck in my throat.

"Maybe we should go home; it looks like it's getting late," I said, wanting to add something else, but Dan interrupted me.

"So, to my place or yours?"

"I'm sorry, what?"

"I'm kidding, darling, I'm kidding. Learn to take a joke."

"Not this kind of joke."

"Okay, whatever. Wait for me by the car; I'll be right back."

He came back quickly, and in fifteen minutes, I was at the dorm. After thanking him, I quickly ran out of the car so that he didn't have time to say anything. But a minute later, I got a text:

"You're so cute. Goodnight, darling."

***

I spent the weekend with my brother again. He asked me how my week was and then pulled out all the details I knew about Dan and everything that happened on the date. When I told him about the fork situation, he vowed to kill him, but Dylan calmly reassured him and said that *he* should do it so that Alex wouldn't get his hands dirty. I looked at them for a few more seconds, expecting them to laugh, but they were serious to the last. I knew I could trust them, and they had always protected me, but this was too much.

We went downtown to a bright and cozy cafe, and each of us got ice cream. Dylan and Alex's tastes are a bit the same, but I can't eat the sour stuff they like. After that, we rushed to the store and bought food for at least three days, knowing what kind of evening we were going to have—the more, the better. We had grand plans: an evening in good company with lots of food and drinks and cool new movies, just like in the old days.

I often thought about Dan, not because I liked him, but rather because I still didn't understand his intentions.

***

On Monday, he asked me out again in front of the whole class, but it was more of an order than a question.

At six, as he wanted, I was ready and waiting for him outside the dorm. His luxury car stood out among the other cars in the parking lot. The interior smelled of smoke—I didn't know he smoked.

"Darling, today if you don't mind, we won't be alone," he said without taking his eyes off the road.

"And with whom?"

"You'll see."

"Then why did you ask me if you've already decided everything?" I asked irritably.

"Who knows, just in case?" he replied with a grin.

We drove into a dark alley between the buildings and continued for about five minutes until we came to an old shop. The windows were broken, which meant that no one was inside. I looked around and wondered if his friends would really come here. Or was it just time for me to pray? But my attempts to start praying were interrupted by the loud creak of the shop door opening.

***

"S'up, mate, you're early today," said the first guy who came out.

"Yeah, for sure. You wanted to see us so badly or something?" said the girl who was hiding behind the first guy, smiling slyly.

"John, Mia, I'm not alone today, as you can see…"

"Is that a problem?" John raised an eyebrow. "D'you wanna?" he asked, pulling out a small plastic bag with white contents from his pocket.

"No."

"Your new flower refuses such a pleasure, quite unexpectedly." His smile grew wider and more dangerous.

"Leave her alone. You can push this stuff elsewhere without any problems."

"Of course, whatever you say, but you're wrong to refuse, kitty," he replied, crossing his arms over his chest as if in a protective gesture.

"I don't think so," Lily said.

"So, we have a kitty with a temper. I suppose if something happens, she can stick her claws into someone's neck."

John had all eyes on him. It was clear what Mia and the guy who hadn't left the shop yet were thinking. They had *God, who am I friends with* written all over them.

"I think it's a good thing to know in case you need a Band-Aid in an emergency—"

He was interrupted by a hard slap on the cheek from Lilith, who was already red in the face. Just as he was about to open his mouth again, Mia slapped him on the back of the head, taking the glass from his hands and the bag from his pocket.

"You've had more than enough for one night."

"You underestimate me; I can have more," he said, reaching for the glass.

"No, you can't, John. Sit down and rest, please. We have guests after all. And please, at least pretend to be sane."

"Oh, easy!" he replied, sitting down on a chair at the entrance.

"You're not alone today. Is she your new girlfriend?" asked the guy who was slowly exiting the shop. He looked the most like Dan among the three, neat and in branded clothes.

"Yes."

"I see," he said, handing each of us a bottle. Dan opened his in a matter of seconds, as if it was not the first time, he had done it and took a sip. Lily, in turn, refused. He made a gesture like 'whatever' and didn't offer it again.

"So, what's the news? What have you been up to while I've been away?"

"Everything is the same. Mia quit her job. I still work as a courier; the money is good, and I'm happy with it. And John is promoting his business. As I said, nothing new. And you?"

"As you can see, there are changes." Dan raised our intertwined fingers and smiled.

"I see, I'm happy for you. And you? Are you happy with your relationship, dolly?"

"Do I have to answer?"

"Wow, I was right when I said that this kitty can make a lace out of your skin with her claws."

"John, calm down already. I asked you to act like a sane, reasonable person."

"I'm trying. What's the problem?"

"The problem is, the girl's eyes could incinerate you."

"Isn't it interesting?" he shouted, crossing one leg over the other.

"No," stated Lilith.

"Lily, would you like some water?" asked Mia.

"Yes, thank you."

***

On the way back, we were silent, and just before I left, Dan asked, "Why did you refuse the bottle? No one would have seen you there."

I answered only with something like, "Alcohol is bad for your health," and closed the car door.

I lay in bed and thought about whether I liked Dan, whether I would ever have sincere feelings for him, and whether he had any feelings for me at all. I didn't want to think that he was just playing with me, that he had strange and very different friends, and that he was strange himself.

The next day, I woke up first, and it was the best start to the day. I didn't have to wait an hour to take a shower. I finished my bathroom routine, took a sip of tea in the kitchen, and ran off to college. A little too fast, but on the other hand, I would have more time to review what I had been studying.

I wasn't surprised when I entered the college and everyone was hustling and looking at me—I didn't care. I wasn't surprised by the girls' sidelong glances and the signs.

"You have climbed too high; it will hurt to fall."

"Witch—you have bewitched him."

"He is just playing with you, don't be happy. You are just a new toy."

I was really surprised by the posters that covered my entire desk—it was something new.

Chapter 7

Dad threw the plate at my brother, hitting Alex in the head. After that, he threw the tray. Alex pressed his hand to his forehead as if trying to seem stronger to our father. Still, the thin line of blood flowing from just above his eye showed the seriousness of the wound. Our father glared at him and then threw the cup he was holding at the wall behind Alex. He didn't miss; it was most likely where he aimed. Once he saw his goal had been fulfilled, he tore his gaze away from my brother and fixed it on the TV, never turning back around. Alex walked to his room, holding the wall with one hand, staggering as the line of blood grew thicker. I saw his legs start to buckle and ran to help him, but only red liquid fell on my hands as if a bucket of paint had been poured on his face. That's when I woke up.

A dream. It was just a dream. I lifted my sleepy hands up and looked at my fingers and under my nails for any traces of blood. Clear—it was really just another damn dream about my father. My hands fell on the blanket like two ropes, and I felt a new surge of heat mixing with cold. There were still two hours before the alarm clock would ring. I didn't dare go back to sleep, so I just went over the events of the previous days in my head.

Had I been offended or hurt by those girls in class? Nah.

Did I start to like Dan? Nope.

Did I like Dan's company? Not really, but as I always say, you shouldn't judge a book by its cover. Maybe they're good people, it's just that their friend is a clown.

***

After only two days, I became immune to all the stupid jokes I heard at college. The way they make fun of me and the way they smirk when someone tries to shut them up could be added to my book. A book is probably an overstatement, but I like it—it pulls me out of bloody nightmares and a sea of curses from time to time. I write it while no one is watching during the night; the text quickly appears on my phone screen as I try to express my thoughts. No one has read it. It is mine and only mine. I've thought about whether I should print it or put it online, but I'm too afraid of criticism. I admit it, my life is in its pages, so criticism of the book would be criticism of my life. It could break me. Not in the literal sense. I am strong, but I'm not sure I would dare to write another line after that.

My character is just like me, a girl who is not very popular in a good way, with a strong character and a difficult past. Am I writing about myself? No, she's different…

***

On Wednesday morning, my friends were running around the room, admiring their appearance before class. It wasn't my type of leisure, so I got up quickly, had breakfast, and headed to college. On the way, there were unusually few people for the hour. It was calm; the cool air curled my hair without my permission. To my right was a busy road, and to my left, lush trees.

My walk was interrupted by Dan, who was beeping his horn like crazy. I ignored him for another six yards until he started sticking his head out of the car and shouting my name, drawing everyone's attention to me. I took a deep breath, exhaled, turned around, opened the car door, and slammed it shut.

***

"You know, you could have closed it gentler."

"Oh, really? I was just following the example of how I was called. What's wrong?"

"Nothing is wrong, dear. You're just too energetic this morning. I wonder where you get your energy from."

Lilith rolled her eyes and turned to him with a tight smile. "Really? Ever heard of 'sleep'? A cool thing, you should try it sometime."

"Thanks, darling, I'll definitely try it. Or do you want to try it together?"

"I'll pass." Lilith grunted.

"As you wish, honey. If you need me, I'm yours 24/7," he sang, and Lily just rolled her eyes.

"Aren't you tired of playing the role of a fool in love?"

"Why the role? Maybe I am madly in love, and that's why I'm acting like a fool."

"A cliché from a low-budget movie."

"Is it really, or maybe my princess is just shy?"

"Keep dreaming."

"I will, darling," Dan answered swiftly.

They exchanged glances, Lilith's was heavy and Dan's was warm, and they rode in silence.

***

Lily wasn't popular among the girls, but the boys were always whispering about her beauty behind her back. In a large group of women, strong women often eliminate the pretty ones. Lily had only three friends, which was enough for a fun life at college. Ever since Dan gave her a lift, the gossip had only intensified. The whispers came from all sides, ranging from compliments about her looks and body proportions to cruel accusations that she was a manipulative girl who charmed guys into liking her.

***

Today is April Fool's. I called it that, summing up the events, though it was just a regular day. Until today, I had complained about the disrespect and bullying because of Dan, but today beat all the records. When I entered the classroom, I saw the familiar insults scrawled on my desk—I was used to them by now. Under the desk, on a second shelf near my things, was someone's sports bag. The moment I pulled it out, a breathless guy ran into the classroom, showering me with accusations before I could even understand what was going on.

***

"HOW DARE YOU! I knew you were like this! God, how stupid I was to defend you against the girls who warned me!" he shouted, his eyes filled with fury as he raked his hand through his hair. "Give me back what you stole!" he demanded, stepping closer, almost hovering over Lilith. A tall, athletic guy, as furious as an angry wolf, could easily scare any girl. At this moment, it was hard to predict what to do—go on the defensive or run away.

"Are you crazy? What are you talking about?" Lilith replied calmly, raising an eyebrow.

"I mean the bag you're shamelessly holding," he shot back.

"What bag? Take it! I found it under the desk," Lilith said, extending the bag, which he nearly tore from her hands.

"Do you really think I'll believe this childish story? Do you know how many times I've heard, 'I didn't take it; it was planted on me,' or, 'Oh, I saw this on my desk and decided to look'? I wonder if that's happened to you too."

"What kind of theater are you putting on? I told you to take it away. Wait, what do you play?"

"What does this have to do with your theft?" he shot back.

"Is it hard to answer?" she pressed.

"No, it's not hard. Basketball."

"Well, then everything's clear. It is obvious—a basketball is heavy. It's hit your head more than once before you got here."

"Are you looking for trouble?"

"And are you trying to intimidate me now? Go ahead, try it! But oops, I'm supposed to be scared of a guy with no evidence or reason. How does that look?"

"You, witch! How am I supposed to wear these clothes now? Where's the guarantee you didn't put anything in there?"

"Oh, I was supposed to put something in there? I just sang it a song and left a drawing as a souvenir," Lilith said, laughing.

"I understand you're having fun now, but we'll see who's laughing when the cops show up. If anything's missing, you'll regret it!" He shot her a concrete glare, but she returned an equally cold, icy look that made him shiver, though he didn't show it.

"See you later," Lilith said with a frosty smile, bringing him back to reality.

"You will pay!" he screamed, storming out of the room like a tornado.

"Sure, sure, whatever you say," she shouted after him, then exhaled and slumped back in her chair, feeling like a squeezed lemon.

Damn, what a way to start the day. Was there really no better prank? Or is this idiot who got hit in the head with basketballs not the only one I have to watch out for today?

The girls, like mosquitoes sensing a target, came rushing toward me, out of breath.

"Lily, the boys said, Nate was here, and he shot out of class like a bullet, fists clenched. They said you could see his jaw muscles working after talking to you. What did he even want?"

"Honestly? I have no idea. Maybe he was looking for someone to help him get his brain back in place—looks like getting hit by that ball knocked it a little sideways."

Her friends laughed.

"You're probably right." Olivia chuckled. "So, what happened? Why did he run away from you like he was set on fire?"

"Set on fire? You must be mixing things up. Ghosts don't go well with fire, but they can definitely leave a frostbite."

"I see you like that nickname," Emma teased.

"I wouldn't say I do, but it's better than what they write about me on the desk. So, girls, from today on, I'll be the coldest and most dangerous ice queen. My goal is to rise above all the gossip surrounding me. What do you think?" Lily smiled.

"You're a badass!"

"Wait, you really are a badass! But what influenced your decision?"

"I don't know, maybe I just got tired of putting up with it," she said deliberately.

"Okay, and where will you start?"

"Make Dan mine?" Lily laughed.

"But he's already yours." Isabelle grinned. "Is there something we don't know about?"

"You're right, he's mine, but unfortunately, not everyone's realized it yet," she said with a predatory smile.

"You really like him?"

Lily replied with a thoughtful smile.

"Really? Since when? No, don't think we have anything against it, but I was sure until the last moment that you'd ice him out. He's cool and all, but not quite your type as I thought," Isabel said, smiling warmly.

"Girls, maybe I'm just used to his advances," she said laughing and skillfully changed the subject.

***

The classes seemed to fly by. After that, my friends and I went to grab our clothes from our lockers. There was a huge crowd, mostly guys. To get there, we had to push through the eye of the storm—there was that dude hit in the head, with half the team next to him. I ignored them, got my stuff from the locker, and closed it. Just then, someone from behind shoved me against the locker, looming over me. It was that jerk. I crossed my arms over my chest, even though he couldn't see it, but I was annoyed, waiting for a reasonable answer to the question, *Why the hell is he wasting my time?*

***

"Where do you think you're going, baby?" he said, adding a mocking twist to the last word.

Lilith turned on her heels to look him in the eye. "If I say, you won't believe." She shrugged.

"What? Have a side job on a pole?" he said laughing, and looked at his friends.

"No, dear, not there," she drawled, running her hand over his shoulder. "But I see you're disappointed by this news. When I have that in mind, I'll let you know. I see you're a regular in such places, and maybe you'll help me out with an interview."

"Easy." He smiled.

"No doubt," she replied in a cold tone. "May I pass?" Lily smiled at him with an angelic grin.

"Not so fast." He pressed her against the door again, creating distance between them. Lily crossed her arms over her chest, and he tensed the arm he was leaning on.

"What else, you want an autograph? I'm not in the mood for any more jokes tonight."

"I hope you're not planning to sign a stolen watch," he shot back with a hard smile. "Where is it?"

"What are you talking about?"

"About the watch that strangely disappeared right after my bag got into your hands."

"Okay, I see we won't solve this situation easily," she muttered under her breath. "So, give me one good reason why I need a man's watch."

"It costs like half your house."

"I suspect that's an overstatement."

"Looked up the price already?"

"I know the value of my house and everything inside it."

"Oh, so you already sold it and bought a luxury house? Guys, did you hear? The girl is going out!"

"Asshole!"

"Yeah? And you must be too stupid to realize the seriousness of the situation."

"Which one? The one where you're picking on me in the middle of the corridor in front of dozens of people? I agree, it's low and disgusting."

"Are you insane? Think about what you're saying," he recoiled, as if scalded.

"Likewise," she said, picking up her things and moving toward the exit. "If you want to accuse me of something, find another way. I'll even wish you good luck with that!" she shouted as she left. Lily walked at a fast pace, seemingly forgetting that the girls had agreed to hang out together.

Fifteen minutes later, she slammed the door to her room, tossed her shoes and bag by the entrance, and headed straight to her wardrobe. Hidden among her clothes was the medicine she desperately needed. Pulling out a single blister, she noticeably calmed down. *It's here, even if it's the last pill.* She popped the pill into her mouth and washed it down with a mug of cold water as if trying to extinguish a fire burning inside her.

"April Fool's for sure… I was ready for pranks and stupid chatter, but getting made a fool of was unexpected," she muttered, rolling over and wrapping herself in the blanket. "We'll see who the puppet master is here."

Chapter 8

In the morning, long before Lily was ready to leave the land of beautiful dreams, her phone decided to draw her attention to itself. It was trying very hard, and Lily picked it up and looked at the screen.

"Hi darling, how are you? I heard you had some problems yesterday. Why didn't you tell me? As your strong, courageous, brave, handsome—oh wait, that's the wrong line… After all, I am an athlete. You thought I wouldn't deal with some little guy?"

"He's not little."

"Are you implying that I couldn't handle him?"

"Quite possibly." She laughed as she typed the message.

"Oh gods, my woman doesn't believe in me. What will I do?"

"I'm not your woman."

"I agree, you are my girl. Oh gods, what did I do wrong in my past life that my sweet, beautiful, and sensitive girlfriend doesn't believe in my strength?"

"Maybe you were not quite a man in your past life? You know, in fact, tiny animals would not have managed such a mission." Lily could not resist and laughed out loud this time.

"Hmm, good thought. If I were your dog, you would instinctively care for me. If I were your plant, you would water me or add fresh soil. But what would you do if I were a mouse or a spider in your house?"

"Oh really, let me think about it. This is a serious question. I believe we have found the one that suits you best. Probably, to begin with, if you were a pest, I would try to drive you out, preferably as soon as possible."

"That reminds me of something."

"I haven't finished typing yet… so if you wouldn't cause any harm, I'd probably keep you…"

"Oh, how romantic, that's how our love story began."

"Oh, come on."

"Okay, okay, so, do you need help with that minor problem today?"

"Why? You said it, it's a minor problem."

"Whatever you say, my queen."

"A queen already?"

"Dear, sweet, gentle, and a little chilly queen, but mine."

Lily did not answer.

This morning started on a good note. There were still two hours before the alarm, and the girl opened her secret document with the text. There, her character was going through a not-so-easy period, which was logical considering that the character and the author shared a lot in common. The shy sixteen-year-old girl is transferred to a new school, where she immediately finds so-called 'enemies' and runs into trouble named 'Rick' who ruins her life and mental stability. The plot is complicated, and

Lilith feels easier when she turns her emotions into a set of letters. It's as if an invisible weight falls from her shoulders, and she breathes out with relief.

***

Before Lily could enter the college, Nate and his friends blocked her path.

"So, what's your plan for apologizing?"

Someone laughed behind Nate.

"I'll definitely think about it when I need to," she replied confidently, looking in his direction.

"Man, she's really either dumb or too brash."

"Lilith Davis, can you spare me some of your time to sort out my problem? As you can see, I have one, and it's not a small one either." He pointed to his hand where the watch used to be.

Lily looked around at all the guys and then slowly turned to look to the clock. "I have thirty minutes to spare. I suggest you watch the video from the cameras in the corridor. Of course, you didn't think of that and are accusing me for no reason."

"Damn! I didn't think of it," he muttered and slapped himself.

"What? I didn't hear you."

"Let's go, I said."

"Lily, is there any trouble?" Dan shouted from the car.

"No, everything is fine, honey." She winked, stupefying Nate.

"Is Dan your boyfriend?" someone asked quietly behind him.

"Yes, why?" Lily raised an eyebrow.

"Nothing, just curious," said the guy, and turned to Nate. "Nate, you better hope it's really her, otherwise we're dead," he whispered into his friend's ear with the same smile, barely moving his lips.

It took some time to convince the guards, but when Nate told them how much the stolen watch was worth, they immediately started rewinding the footage from the moment the school opened. The footage showed lots of people walking down the corridor, but no one entered Lily's classroom. Two of her girl classmates came in with small bags that wouldn't fit Nate's uniform, followed by a guy, and then three more. Then Lily appeared with her stylish little bag that couldn't even fit her notebooks. She could have replaced it with her old one, but this one was dearer to her—it was a birthday present from Alex and Dylan.

***

Having watched the video twice before Nate came in angry looking for his uniform, we concluded that there was a possibility that it had been dropped off a day before. We had to watch the video of the previous day in its entirety until the school closed, which took a lot of time even with rewinding. I noticed that I was already late for my first class. However, it was not for nothing. Twenty minutes before the school closed, in the darkness of the corridors under the moonlight, the silhouette of a man, perhaps a boy, creeps into the classroom. He quietly and very slowly opens the door and goes inside, and in about two minutes, he comes out. The guy was wearing a hoodie covering his face, although, for a moment, he was caught by one camera while turning to the opposite side of the corridor, though not very clearly. Apparently, he didn't know about the existence of that camera.

We spent another five minutes zooming in on his face at different timestamps to get a better picture. When the photo was ready, a quick and loud knock brought me out of my thoughts. I turned and saw that one of the guys who had been keeping a distance was lying on the floor, and Nate was hovering over him, clenching his fist.

***

"What the fuck, huh? I didn't expect a rat among my friends."

"Nate, wait, listen, I had no choice, I needed the money," the guy said, breathing heavily and slowly backing away.

"Money? Are you serious? You just had to ask!"

"It was too much."

"Oh, I see. Stealing it was easier. Well done, but why did you plant it on her?" Nate nodded his head toward Lily.

"Because no one likes her anyway, so no one would be surprised if she had done something like this."

“I see,” Nate said, getting up. “Well, that’s fun,” he continued, shaking off the dirt. “I advise you to tell me what you needed the money for.”

And he did, without details, but enough so that everyone could understand.

“Excuse me, I guess I can go now.” Lilith snapped them out of their trance. She was already standing at the door with a bored look, arms crossed over her chest.

“Yes, you can go,” one of the guys said.

“Don’t you have anything to say?”

“For example?” one of them asked, surprised.

“For example, ‘I’m sorry we were wrong. Oh, it really wasn’t you. I’m sorry we delayed you, and you almost missed the first class you’d been preparing for hours…’ maybe something like that?” She laughed.

“I’m sorry,” Nate said quietly.

“That’ll do. I’m going to run off now. You’ll figure out the rest yourselves.”

***

On the way to the classroom, I remembered that I now have a class with a teacher who loves me as much as I love him, and this thought made me a little uneasy. But in front of the classroom door, I managed to regain control of my emotions.

“Good morning, sorry I’m late. I was helping a friend find a stolen watch.”

“Morning. Ms. Davis, as I understand it, you’ve picked the wrong program. But it’s fine, a few more absences and you can choose something new after you're expelled."

"I'm sorry I'm late. I can tell you about our homework topics. I've been preparing."

"Oh, no, Lilith Davis, you can't. I understand if you're a minute or two late, five at the most. But it's already twenty minutes before the end. You've already got a mark for truancy on your record today. If you want, sit down and listen, or you can continue practicing your future profession, I don't care."

"I'm sure I'll have time to answer the questions you gave us for homework. Please give me a chance."

"No, you've already lost it. Don't waste the whole class's time."

"After the class, could you stay for a few minutes?"

"No. Don't waste my time either. I'll see you at the exam, Miss Davis. There we'll find out how well you prepared."

Chapter 9

"Meet me after school today, honey?"

"Let's meet now, I'm free. How about you?"

"In a moment! I'll wait by the car, or do you want to walk?"

"Let's walk around the city. I'm heading to the main entrance."

"Ten minutes and I'll be there for you, sunshine."

Ten minutes later, Dan was really there. She could only imagine how he had escaped from his last class. Without asking, he took Lily's hand and led her to the exit.

"Where are you planning to go?"

"I don't know, I just want to get my mind off things..."

"I have an idea, though it's not the best time, but it's worth a look," he said, holding her hand gently as they walked through streets that were not quite familiar to her. They had long since passed the college, the familiar café, and the park, moving as if to the very edge of the city. After an hour, Lily felt weak, tired, and a slight pain in her feet, as if to warn her that it could be worse if she didn't change her shoes.

Perhaps Dan noticed something in her walk, so near the nearest shop, he suggested she sit down on a bench. "Wait here, I'll be right back."

Lily shook her head in response and sat on the bench with one leg stretched out in front of her, the other bent at the knee. The air was fresh, filled with the strong smell of pine needles.

"Here." He held out a bottle of water. "Straighten your leg, please."

"Thank you… Wait, what for?" She raised her eyebrows.

"You'll see."

Lily listened and Dan quickly took off both shoes from her feet, examined the wounds, wiped them with a damp cloth, and applied a Band-Aid.

"Are you serious, Dan? Thanks for buying them, but I could have done it myself." She blushed, feeling embarrassed by the situation.

"Of course, you could, but what's so strange about me wanting to take care of my girlfriend?" He smiled warmly and sat down next to her. "By the way, I have something else for you."

"Something else? You scare me, dear." She laughed.

"I hope I've guessed the right taste," he said, holding out the condensed milk ice cream.

"You did absolutely well," she chirped, tasting the dessert.

"Will there be a reward?" he asked sincerely, doing his best not to laugh.

"We'll see."

"So, I'm not hopeless?"

"As you can see, no."

"That's great."

They sat on a bench outside a small shop near the forest until Lily finished her dessert.

"Are you ready to go on? We have about ten more minutes to go. If not, I'll call a taxi and we'll go somewhere else," he said, waiting for an answer without taking his eyes off her.

"I can do it."

"Are you sure?"

"Yes, I want to see what you so sincerely want to show me," she said with a smile, looking into his eyes.

***

The small forest just behind the shop was quiet and peaceful as we walked up the spiral path, paved with stones, leading uphill through the trees. We didn't encounter many people on the way; perhaps it was not yet the hour when everyone else wanted to enjoy the silence.

When the trail ended, Dan took me to a small concrete platform with benches along the edge of the fence. He led me closer to the edge, and I was breathless—the whole city lay beneath my feet, everything appearing small and close. For the first time, I saw the entire city: the amusement park, the university, the river, and the park nearby with people playing and swimming. I was overwhelmed with emotions, unable to react when Dan ran his hand through my hair and, without breaking eye contact, gently pulled me closer to him. He tenderly stroked my cheek with his thumb and held my other hand in his. In a quick, frantic moment, I felt his lips meet mine, awkwardly at first, as if seeking permission for a kiss. It was brief, but his warmth and taste remained on my lips.

***

"You look beautiful today."

"Thank you, Dan," Lilith replied, stepping back a little. "It's really beautiful here, now I understand why you wanted to bring me here."

"I'm glad you're happy. You know, Lily, I can't stop thinking about you," he replied with a slight smile, not letting go of Lilith's hand, and the girl blushed terribly.

"Really?" She looked up shyly.

"Of course. I used to be different; you've probably heard the gossip and everything, but you know, you're like a treasure I've been searching for—a treasure that was meant to change me."

Who can explain that feeling when your heart is tap-dancing in your chest and your soul is having fun on a trampoline?

***

They descended much faster than they had gone up, and half of the way to the car, Dan carried Lily on his back as the sores on her legs became unbearable. She leaned against him, feeling the warmth that was so new yet so comforting. Dan's favorite music played in the car, filling the space with a comfy atmosphere. There were moments when Lily sang along, and Dan tapped his fingers to the rhythm of the music on the steering wheel.

"Thank you for today… you really managed to cheer me up, despite the fact that I'll have problems with my exam," she said in a disgruntled tone and leaned back.

"Didn't you prepare?" he asked.

"I did. I was ready for the class, but I was late because I was helping one of the guys to find his watch."

"Did you find it?" he asked, eyes on the road.

"Yeah."

"Well, that's good news. Consider it a tick in the karma box, and the exam is just a small formality."

"I hope so," she said smiling.

"Do you want a ride home, sweetie?"

"No, you can stop somewhere in the center. I'll walk myself. You're going the other way."

"Okay. So, what did he do in class this time?"

"You mean the teacher? He insisted that I'll pass everything on the exam and not waste his time."

"Should I consider him a competitor?"

"Are you kidding?"

"No, tell me, will anyone else have problems like this?"

"Probably not."

"You see. So, I'll be there with you." He chuckled.

"Okay, but if something goes wrong, you'll have to clean it up, my love."

"Of course." He squeezed her hand, a cheeky smile on his face.

"You can stop here."

"Okay."

"Where are you going?" She turned to him, furrowing her brows.

"It's better to make a U-turn here."

"Oh, okay. Wait, are you going to turn or not?"

"I will. Near your dorm."

"How unexpected."

"And nice?"

"Yeah."

"Will you kiss me goodbye?"

"Keep on dreaming." She snorted.

"And on the cheek, at least once."

She squinted her eyes, searching his. "Okay, just one."

It was a brief kiss, but as warm as a cafe latte.

***

At home, I immediately opened my book, and words gradually began to appear on a blank white page, describing adventures, incredible landscapes, a lot of pleasant emotions, and the kiss that ended the chapter. It wasn't like my kiss; it was sensual, long, and tender—just like I imagined it.

That night, I felt neither hunger nor pain. I slept soundly, dreams overlapping every few hours until morning. Olivia woke me up, her not-so-happy expression suggesting she had left her warm bed against her will. While listening to her complain about how heartless Emma was for interrupting such a beautiful dream she had,

I seized the chance to dash into the bathroom before Olivia. That was my little morning victory.

Walking alone to college wasn't as sad as it might seem; I felt comfortable. The sun, not yet fully awake, bid farewell to the moon, which squinted toward the bright sun and gradually disappeared. Many people passed me: children off to school, bewildered adults likely late for work. The air carried scents of dust, flowers, greenery, people's perfume, and a faint hint of incense trailing an elderly woman, perhaps just from church, I thought, heading to college.

Today, we had practical classes. The task: to conduct engaging educational lessons for children at neighboring schools. Topics were assigned beforehand, and lesson plans were submitted for review the day before. My first lesson was with fourth graders on 'Modern Storytelling Based on Classic Fairy Tales.' The children's eyes lit up when I mentioned they could base characters on figures like Aurora, Ariel, Stella, Muse, or Draculaura for girls, and Naruto, Sasuke, Luffy, or Meliodas for boys. Their stories turned out to be interesting. Each of them intertwined everyday life with fantasy, and the rich imagination of the children was shining through them.

My second lesson was with tenth graders, and if I was nervous before the fourth graders, now I sat confidently pulling out the lesson plan with class 10B? Topic… 'How to Count to Ten'? Desperation wasn't the word to describe my feelings then; my face was hot, my body like cotton, especially seeing how quickly the students settled in. I should have been prepared for this. Yes, I should have, but who on earth leaves the house preparing to be hit by a car? Okay, it wasn't the first time. Maybe they were playing a game, testing me to see my reaction. Well, let's see what happens next.

"Good morning, everyone," I greeted, standing confidently with the lesson plan in hand. I pushed aside my panic and fear; my hands weren't shaking enough for anyone to notice. Today, I'm a teacher, so I have to be competent.

"Good morning," the class replied.

"Today, we're going to have a rather unusual lesson. How often do you talk to your teachers about issues that bother you in everyday life, school, family?"

"Not often, sorry, but what does this have to do with the lesson topic?"

"The direct topic of today's lesson is 'How to Count to Ten,' or how not to stop at the first obstacle."

"An interesting topic."

The class chuckled.

"I agree, and it's a real-life topic. So, tell me, how often do you stop yourself in class when you know the right answer? Or how often are you afraid to ask a passerby for directions, or your parents or teachers for advice?"

"Okay, let's say some of us do. So what?"

"It's just that right now, you're at the stage where the first obstacle in a task might stop you. During this lesson, I want to prove to you that the first obstacle isn't always as difficult as it seems at first glance."

"Okay, you've got us interested. But what about the topic that's on our schedule?"

"Isn't the life lesson more important? Besides, it's in my plan, so I don't see any problem."

After these words, the class fell silent for a few seconds, thinking, and then an outpouring of questions and examples of situations followed. We collectively analyzed and discussed them, with even the shyest students participating.

By the end of the lesson, the students had mixed emotions. They enjoyed the lesson and were sad that there wouldn't be more like it. We agreed to meet again sometime, leaving the classroom on a positive note.

Chapter 10

"Hi, cutie, I've been waiting for you for thirty minutes. What has taken you so long?"

"Nothing important; I had to stay longer with the teacher," Lily said as she fastened her seat belt.

"And why did he delay you for so long?" Dan asked, raising a defiant eyebrow.

"Just to find out why I was teaching a different lesson than the one he had planned."

"And why is that?"

"I taught the lesson according to the plan I received from the class monitor right before the lesson. I didn't have time to review it, and I don't regret changing the topic. I think today's lesson was useful to them."

"So, they wanted to set you up?" Dan's eyebrow twitched slightly, but the girl didn't let it slip.

"I guess so, but as you can see, their plans melted like snow in the spring. By the way, where are we going?" Lily asked in surprise as if she had just realized that her home was on the other side of town.

"To my friend's house," he said smiling.

"And you didn't even ask me if I wanted to go with you?" Lily blurted out, crossing her arms over her chest and leaning back in her seat.

"I knew you'd like the idea."

"I hope it's not the same friends as last time," she said thoughtfully, looking out the window.

"You'll see," Dan said, and his smile grew wider.

On the way in the car, Lily was texting her friends, telling them about the ridiculousness of the situation. Despite how absurd she described it, she liked Dan's attention, and nice gifts or secret trips can interest absolutely any woman. Olivia talked about her new clothes, mentioning that she passed by a shop with cool cosmetics the other day but didn't buy anything, so today she had to catch up on both times. Isabella just commented on their messages; apparently, she had no news yet.

Meanwhile, Emma sent:

"Wish me luck today."

"What are you planning to do today?"

"I plan to make one of the cutest guys in our college fall in love with me."

"Wow, what a goal! And who is this lucky guy?"

"Nate Wilson."

"Wait, is this the same Nate I was squeezing an apology from?"

"Yep."

"Okay, so how come you're going on a date?"

"It's not a date."

"Okay, so how come you two are going out outside of college?"

"It's simple. I approached him during a break to ask if he had a girlfriend, and he said he was free. So, I decided not to miss this great opportunity and asked him to meet me."

"And what did he say?"

"Yes, okay, sure, no problem… something like that. I'm not sure he understood me correctly, so today I'll have to give it my best shot."

"Doing what, if not a secret?"

"Well, at least being patient. I plan to listen to him talk about basketball for two hours. How do you think I'll manage?"

"Chances are above average."

"Well, at least something."

"With your looks, I wouldn't worry at all."

"Isabella, are you saying I shouldn't hope for anything, or that just the sight of my lips will blow his mind?"

"You're pushing yourself too hard, girl."

"Of course, I haven't had a date in a long time."

"But this is not a date, right?"

"Yes! Enough, you're confusing me. Lily, do you have a long way to go?"

"Dan says five more minutes and we'll be there."

"Great, good luck, have a nice day and all that. I'm going to go get my clothes ready."

"Thank you. You too."

"And she calls it not-a-date," Isabella commented.

"Yeah, lol. Okay, I'm out too."

"Bye."

***

Dan stopped at a dark house that did not stand out from the others on the street. The street itself was in the center of the city, but it looked abandoned and dead as if the last time a human had set foot on it had been at least ten years ago. Lily got out of the car and closed the door behind her, and the place was silent. Dan wordlessly held out his hand to Lily, a gesture she could not refuse given the pitch blackness. They walked around the house and came to the stairs on the other side of the house, which led downstairs. Dan took a few steps forward, pulled the key out of his pants, and opened the door with a quick movement.

The dark corridor ended with another pair of doors which he opened again without any problems, easily, as if he had been training almost every day. The corridor was filled with bright light, and it took Lily a few seconds to realize where it was coming from. Dan led her into the hall, a large and spacious room, in the center of which were tables, people sitting at them with cards in their hands, waiters carrying glasses of alcohol. All around them, people were gambling.

"Surprised?"

"Am I surprised that you've brought me to some illegal casino? No, of course not; how could I be surprised?" Lily said, looking around the room and assessing the situation.

"This is our bar."

"What do you mean?"

"My friends and I put it together piece by piece. At first, it was just anyone interested in our product and willing to pay the price. Now it's just the elite. To win the attention of influential people, we had to work hard. But as they say, if you know where to look for the money, the money will find you. After we opened the casino, we not only learned to look for the money but also to manage it well."

"It's interesting, of course, but I don't see the point of why you brought me here. I'm not the elite, and I'm not interested in your goods," she replied with a smile.

"Consider yourself part of the club. Let's go." Dan gently grabbed Lily's hand and pulled her to the far door at the end of the hall.

"Oh, hello, mate. Not expected. You know how to surprise. I see you brought your flower too," John shouted at them.

"Hi, as you can see," he replied, taking the glass from his hands.

"Beautiful little bud, would you like to try our drink this time?" John smiled playfully at her.

"I'll pass, thanks," Lily said with a look of disgust.

"Why is it that people from all over the country come here and pay all the money in the world for it, and I offer it to you for nothing, and you still refuse?"

"That's right, I refuse." Lily held his gaze.

"Oh, this is not just a kitty cat; this is a real tigress. I'm afraid if I continue, she will spill my glass." He smiled at her as he raised his glass.

"Aren't you afraid I'll scratch your eyes out? You know not all cats like it when you look in their eyes so brazenly."

"What do you mean, little flower?" he teased.

"A look as if someone wants to eat them; that's why there is an irresistible desire to sharpen claws. What do you think?" She smiled at John, who immediately put his glass away from his mouth with interest.

"Boy, I told you the other day that she was a real treasure. This time I'll tell you that I envy you."

"Wipe away the drool; it's already on your chin."

"Oh, my God, you noticed?" John asked with an innocent look.

"Sure, mate, sure." Dan tapped him on the shoulder as he sat down next to him.

"I see you're in a good mood today," Mia said.

"I'd say great," John replied, taking another sip.

"I can see that. Lily, would you like something to drink?" Paul asked.

"No, thanks."

"Not from our menu. Something ordinary?"

"Do you have water?"

"I'll get it," he said and quietly went into the other room.

"And what do you do here, if not a secret? To be honest, at first glance, it was hard to tell that you have such achievements in life."

"I agree. On weekends and some weekdays, guys are like drunks who are so in love with their glass that they are ready to part with it only at gunpoint—that is, never—so they can often be found sleeping in an embrace with bottles," Mia said with a serious expression.

"Mia, that was classified information!" John shouted.

"Sure, but you may have forgotten, she already has the pass." The girl laughed, infecting the company with laughter.

"Oh shit, so she'll soon know all my secrets?"

"Of course, she will, honey."

"Damn!" he shouted. "And about the incident in the bathroom?"

"About it as well," Mia continued.

"And even about the situation in the mountains?"

"Of course," she answered, barely restraining herself.

"No, it's not fair," John thought seriously.

"You'll short-circuit your main processor soon. Spare your not-so-big-for-your-age brain," Paul interrupted him as he entered the room with two glasses of water.

"And how do you know its size?"

"Unfortunately, my friend, it is noticeable," he said with a heavy breath.

"John, there is a client," a voice came from the hall.

"I'm coming. It's a pity that such a pleasant and interesting conversation was interrupted. Unfortunately, I have to go. Will you miss me?"

"Of course, we will." Mia laughed.

"That's good to hear."

***

The rest of the evening flew by. Dan and Mia were actively discussing something, Paul stuck to his phone, and John came over to talk to me from time to time, but he was called to the hall too often, so maybe it was for the best.

I don't remember the last half hour very well; I was very sleepy. I know that Dan woke me up outside the dormitory, and I said goodbye to him and went up to my room. It was already dark outside, and after texting my brother that I was fine and in my room, I fell asleep right away.

***

"Wake up, Sleeping Beauty," Emma shouted across the room.

"What time is it?" Lily asked, rubbing her eyes.

"Class starts in an hour," Isabelle said smiling, holding a pepper packet up to Olivia's nose.

"Oh crap, the alarm didn't go off?" Lily asked, pulling on her trousers.

"It did, and repeatedly," Isabelle answered, just after Olivia had said a few 'loving' words to her.

"So, how was your evening? Why did you come back so late?" Emma asked, holding out a mug of tea.

"You didn't—"

"No sugar; I remember."

"Thanks. To be honest, it was nothing special. He took me to a place where they often get together with friends. I already knew them, so it wasn't that difficult. Well, I have nothing else to tell, so tell us how you're doing," Lily said, smiling at her.

"And you don't want to tell us anything in detail? Did you think that by saying you are doing well you would get rid of us?"

"Girls, to be honest, I'm still trying to understand everything that's happening there. I'll say crime is involved—not murders or anything like that. The place is secret, but the elite hang out there."

"Since when did you learn to talk in riddles? And what are we supposed to understand from this?" Isabelle asked impatiently.

"Just leave it. She's already explained everything clearly. The place is closed off; it's full of elites, criminals, and big money. So, it's better if we don't know anything about it," Emma explained to her friend.

"You're right..." Lily whispered as she packed her things into her bag.

"All right, fine, you want to know how my date went? I'll tell you how it went." Emma paused theatrically until she had everyone's attention. "We walked through the city at night, drank hot chocolate, and he took me to a park where we sat for a long time. Honestly, it was an interesting meeting; he's completely different from the rude jerk he first seemed to be."

"Sounds nice. How did your walk end?"

"With a kiss, of course," Emma chirped.

"Can I ask, who kissed whom?"

"It was the last minute of our walk. It was dark outside, and a cold wind was blowing occasionally, chilling us to the bone."

"Can you get to the point?"

"Don't interrupt! We were sitting on the ground under a big tree, with the moon peeking at us through the branches. It was romantic. He extended his hand to help me up, and next to him, I felt so small and protected."

"Sure, sure, more than a foot difference. So, what happened next?"

"Then there was a kiss, and after that, he walked me home."

"Wait, so who kissed whom first?" Lily asked excitedly.

"I kissed him, of course."

"For some reason, I'm not surprised." Isabel exhaled with relief.

"Well, you know guys; you can't expect them to make the first move."

"Exactly, so you decided to take matters into your own hands. Got it."

"Good mo-orning," Olivia said, yawning as she came out of the bathroom. "Did I miss anything?"

"No, dear, nothing important. All you missed was how Lily was at a criminal party with the elite and how Emma kissed a guy. Nothing new, right? Anyway, I'm heading out. Who's coming with me?"

"Wait, I'm coming too."

"And me."

"Wa-ait, I need details!"

Chapter 11

"Hi, Lily, how are you?"

"Hi, Dylan, same as always. How about you? What's up?"

"We're just getting ready for my birthday party, which is why I'm calling, by the way. Will you come over tomorrow?"

"No need to ask! Of course, I will! Who else is coming?"

"Only the closest ones. Panther members and their loved ones."

"Oh, I feel it will be interesting. So, what time are you gathering everybody?" Lilith eagerly ran her hands through her hair, her eyes sparkling with curiosity.

"Everyone is going to the party at six, so we'll pick you up at half past six if you agree."

"My big brother is afraid that I won't make it on my own?" She giggled.

"Yeah, believe me, Alex is really afraid."

She laughed into the phone.

"It's not surprising."

"Yeah, well, it was good to hear you. See you later."

"Bye."

***

Great, so this year Dylan is celebrating with the Panthers. They used to be on one school team, but who would have thought that after so many years their friendship would not disappear. I didn't spend much time thinking about the gift, but I guess I should have. This year I will give Dylan a matching pair of tracksuits. I think he and my brother will be happy.

I grew up around the Panthers since I was a little girl. After my father died, my brother and I only had them left, and the Panthers seemed to feel the same connection to us. We lived with Dylan for a while, and his grandmother still treats us with homemade delights from time to time. Some time ago, Dylan's older siblings were ready to throw us out on the street just to keep us out of sight. But Dylan was able to quickly put everything in its place, and Grandad—that is, Dylan's father—was on our side. Despite the fact that from the very start, it was difficult for him to accept his son's relationship, everything is fine now. I'm glad it ended this way. I'm glad my brother found himself a good guy, and I'm glad Dylan's family was understanding about their relationship.

After Dylan announced his relationship with my brother in front of the entire company—even if that meant he could be removed from the list of candidates for inheritance and the company, he didn't care; his relationship was more important—his father had no choice but to accept it with a clear mind. Now I feel like I have two older brothers. It's a really cool feeling when you know that you can be protected if something happens.

The car arrived just in time. I wore a lilac dress, that emphasized my waist, and white shoes, and I carried the gift wrapped in white paper with a delicate lilac ribbon. Dylan's house was as impeccable as ever, like a palace that could easily accommodate two hundred people.

On the way, I had this feeling—hmm, how to describe it?—like butterflies in my stomach dancing hip-hop. Such an interesting feeling… I'm really looking forward to meeting the Panthers.

***

Lily got out of the car and saw a small sparrow flying overhead. It was beautiful and very small, and it gave her a little time to catch her breath. *I'm ready! I really want to see them!*

"Oh, is that our little Lily?" a lady said happily, carrying the glasses to the table.

"Oh yeah! It's amazing how fast kids grow up," said another lady next to her.

"Do you think my daughter will grow up this fast too? I mean, it's great, but I don't want her to grow up so fast. Jason, she won't grow up so fast, will she?"

"No, honey."

"Phew, that's good."

"So, our baby Lily is not a baby anymore, but a real girl?"

"I hear our little girl has a boyfriend now, some sort of rich kid."

"I'm glad to see you too, and since you've already dug up a lot about me, I have the right to ask you too…" She paused while everyone was quiet in anticipation. "Mary, how is your relationship with David? Is there anything new?" Lily looked over. "Amy, how's Gary's career going? Alice, I haven't seen your daughter for a long time. When are you going to visit?"

"All's great, no changes." Mary rubbed the back of her head.

"Steadily good; nothing new," Amy said laughing.

"You mean steadily different?"

"Yeah." She smiled.

"Alice?"

"I think we can come over this weekend. I'd like to, and our little sweetie has been asking about you lately. I have an idea—maybe you can ask Jason the same question." She looked with cat eyes.

"Okay, where are the boys?"

"Well, we're keeping the old traditions alive. Alex, Dylan, Leo, and Eric are pouring drinks, and the rest are outside cooking at the barbecue."

"I hope this year will be without incident and the fire department will rest easy," Lily said, crossing her fingers.

"Let's hope so."

***

A pleasant aroma of fried vegetables and meat, and something burnt, was coming from the street to the house. But when we asked the boys if everything was okay, they immediately covered the barbecue with their bodies and nodded politely in agreement.

As I predicted, Dylan liked my gift. Well, he didn't say it directly, but the fact that thirty minutes later, both my brother and he were wearing my gift was a sign. Everyone appreciated the matching tracksuits, especially Leo, who was one of the first to know about the connection of these two.

***

"When will you be home?"

"I'm staying at my brother's tonight."

"Really, at your brother's?"

"Is this your attempt at humor? Or are you trying to ruin my mood right now?"

"Who knows? You're my girlfriend, that's why I'm worried that you're not sleeping at home, but in a house with a bunch of guys."

"Yeah, a bunch of guys who have become like older brothers to me in recent years."

"Yeah, a lot of guys say that, and then they don't understand the words 'we're just friends' and that a relationship is impossible."

"Are you finished? I see you're very bored."

"Of course I'm bored. You're far away. I'm worried. I didn't go anywhere today. You know how hard it is to sit alone at home when your significant other is at a party ALONE."

"Oh, so you're upset that you're not with me? I'm sorry, I think it's too early to introduce you to the brothers."

"Do you doubt my feelings? Do you not believe that they are sincere and strong?"

"Come now, I believe our love story can *surpass* even that of Romeo and Juliet, darling."

"Oh, indeed, my Juliet, wouldst thou not like to join me for a little feast my family is hosting?"

"O, Romeo, shall not thy family be against a lowborn lass with neither influential name nor noble birth?"

"Of course not, my dear Juliet, and even if they were, I would never set foot in that house again!"

"Oh, darling, why say such things? It is your family. I am not worth it."

"Let them try, if the earth be not dear to them, to speak ill of my love."

"My love, what kind of evening shall it be? A banquet or merely an assemblage?"

"It will be a banquet for prominent families. My father intends to find new partners, and my grandmother to confirm her status. So darling, will you come?"

"You have left me with a difficult choice. Will there be many guests? And if I present myself poorly, would I disgrace you because of that?"

"Fear not, Juliet. I shall be there, and if thou tire of the treats, thou shalt not leave the banquet alone."

"Okay, I'll take your word for it."

"Excellent. Then I must count the hours until our next meeting, my Juliet."

“Wait, hours, you say? And when exactly will that banquet be?”

“Oh, the fairy of dreams hath visited me early today, my dear, lovely Juliet. How wouldst thou feel about hearing all when we see each other again?”

“Fine, go to sleep now.”

“Thou art cruel, but thy spirit is like a pearl found at the bottom of the sea.”

“Listen, go to bed already, because your conversation style resembles a fever dream right now.”

“That’s all love.”

“God, why are you so cruel to him?”

***

I slept that night on the second floor in my very well-known room. As morning approached, the music and noise faded, and when I opened my eyes again, it was completely quiet.

I was pulled out of a rather interesting dream, that I could not remember after waking up, by a knock on the door. I heard the familiar sounds of footsteps, and without opening my eyes, I could tell that my brother was bringing me breakfast. I threw back the blanket and sat up. Alex put a cup of hot tea on the table next to me and the treats in the middle of the bed. He has this habit of eating in bed.

***

"How are you? What's new at college? How's your Dan?" Alex obviously restrained his disgust at the last words.

"I'm fine. College is interesting. I have a lot of friends, and things with Dan seem to be working out. It's a shame you haven't got to know him properly. I think you'd like him."

"You think so?" He raised one eyebrow.

"I'm sure. He's liked by everyone he talks to. Maybe he has some kind of magic," Lily said innocently.

"Anything is possible. I'm just wondering how you fell for him so easily."

"Alex! Don't talk like that. Let's change the subject," she said, eating a cookie.

"Okay, how are you feeling? You ate a lot of things yesterday that are on the 'not recommended' list for your illness," he said, handing his sister some tea.

"I have a little burning sensation, but it's not as bad as you imagine," Lilith replied, sticking her tongue out at him and finally taking the tea in her hands.

"Maybe we should go to the hospital. I'm not forcing you to get checked out or anything; we can just go and talk to the doctor. What do you think, Lily?" he asked, waiting patiently for his sister's answer.

"Alex, don't worry. The situation is not so critical now, but I promise you that if anything comes up, I'll call you right away."

"Deal!" Alex said with enthusiasm. "You know, about eight years ago, I was sure I wouldn't be able to replace our parents for you and raise you alone. Now that you've grown up, I see how much you resemble our mom, and I think she would have wanted to be your best friend. What a pity that life is so cruel. She was like an angel. How could such a beautiful, sweet, and intelligent woman choose our father? He is the biggest bastard I have ever seen! The only thing I can thank him for is that at least he didn't kick us out of the house after our mother's death."

"I'm still afraid to go to the guest room in the evening. I know it's just my imagination, but I have a feeling that he is still there, in the same place as before, with a cup or a bottle in his hand that could fly at you at any moment..."

"Do you dream about him?"

"Yes, and it's often," she said, taking a big sip of tea. "I often go over our past in my head and in my dreams, I relive the moments when you were in the hospital because of him every time."

"You know he's not there anymore, Lily. He's gone, and all our troubles are gone. It won't change our terrible past, but it will definitely make us stronger. Not all children worked from childhood, begged, and regularly received slaps from their fathers. Even though he doesn't deserve to be called a father, those few years with him made us strong," Alex said, kissing Lily's forehead. "I can see that you have a lot on your mind right now, and I understand that there are things you just don't want to talk about. But you know I'm here for you anyway, to help you out with something or to get rid of someone from your field of view. Just remember that. And don't take all the little things too personally. Your stomach is alive too, and it's worried about you."

Lily smiled back as she washed down another cookie with tea. "You know, about Dan… How to say it correctly? I still do not understand what kind of person he is. He sincerely chirps to me about love, but in situations where I need at least minimal help, his enthusiasm is below zero. He wants to introduce me to his family, although when he introduced me to his friends, he didn't say a word to make it easier for me to get acquainted."

"And yet you like him?"

"Yes, I guess."

"Well, for now, that's the most important thing. I'll be honest, I didn't like your Dan right away, and even now I can't say that I've taken a liking to him, but it's your choice. I won't try to change it."

"Thank you."

Chapter 12

David and Mary dropped me off at my dorm, and after changing, I fell face-first into the pillow. Seriously, what kind of relationship do Dan and I even have? I tried distracting myself from those stupid thoughts in various ways. I opened my book, wrote two lines, and closed it—I just wasn't in the mood for writing. There are days when you want to write, but the words just won't come. I made myself a cup of tea and opened the book I had been reading on my phone earlier, thinking it might be a good way to distract myself. It was useless. The book felt heavy like it physically weighed a ton. Every page was a struggle like I was dragging that weight on my shoulders. At least the tea was good.

***

"You don't have any plans this evening, do you, my dear Juliet?"

The first thing that came to mind was how well telepathy works nowadays—or maybe he's set up hidden cameras in my room. But I still hope he's being rational.

"I'm free. Why do you ask?"

"Well, today's the banquet we talked about, the one my family is organizing. I want you to be there too, my love."

"So unexpected. I didn't expect it to be so soon."

"Are you refusing? Please, don't break my heart."

"Wait, but what will I wear? I didn't prepare at all."

"Don't worry about it; I took care of the clothes. Trust me."

"Okay! How long will it take?"

"Just say the word, and we'll be out of there."

"Okay."

"Great, I'll be there in an hour."

"So soon?"

"I'll bring your clothes, jewelry, and shoes. I know a lady needs time to get ready—I'll give you plenty of it."

"Oh, my Romeo, you know exactly what a girl needs."

"I'll take that as a compliment."

***

An hour later, just as Dan had promised, an exquisite black evening dress lay on my bed, paired with equally dark and charming shoes. A box with a necklace and earrings awaited me on the table. The jewelry was delicate, with heavy, expensive stones that looked exquisite against the thin lines of silver. I put on the dress, shoes, and earrings myself, but Dan insisted on fastening the necklace, saying it was a family heirloom meant for his future wife. He said it was a kind of ritual as if I was already stepping into that role.

On the way to the banquet, I caught a glimpse of a box in the back seat of the car, a clear sign that Dan had been planning this evening for a while. He looked like he'd just stepped off a red carpet—'exquisite' was the only word that came to mind. I must have been speechless, taking in the expensive watch, the stylish suit, the perfectly done hairstyle that likely came from the best salon, all of it accentuated by a long-lasting, attractive cologne that seemed to declare: "I am the main character here."

***

The house was enormous, far too big for this city—it seemed to occupy the entire center. White with a sprawling garden and paths lined with evergreen trees, it was both impressive and intimidating. As we approached the main entrance, I noticed a parking lot on the side of the house filled with cars whose value I couldn't even begin to imagine. We were greeted by a man in a suit, a slight smile crossing his lips when he saw Dan, but the moment his eyes landed on me, he quickly composed himself and led us inside with a serious expression.

I felt dizzy. No, really—dazed. There were so many people, faces I'd only seen on the internet or on magazine covers. But that wasn't the worst part. The worst came when Dan's grandmother approached to meet us.

***

"My sweetheart, I'm so glad to see you! How are you? Why are you alone?" she chirped, her eyes closely inspecting her grandson. She hugged him, smoothing out the strands that had escaped from his neat hairstyle.

"Grandma, you may not have noticed yet, but I'm not alone today," he said with a smile, stepping aside to reveal Lily standing before the lady of the house.

"Oh, really? It's nice to meet you, young lady." She smiled briefly at Lily before turning her gaze back to her grandson.

"I'm glad to meet you too," Lily replied.

"Are you? That's nice. By the way, Dan, Nataly has been waiting for you in the main hall for an hour already. Go say hello and catch up with your cousins," she directed in a sweet tone, her smile never faltering as she addressed Lily, "We'll chat for a bit."

"Will you be okay?" Dan asked Lily. "I'll be right back," he added, winking at her.

"Okay," Lily whispered after him, doing her best to withstand the intense gaze that seemed to burn through her.

"Now, let's get down to business before the other guests see you. How much do you want?" the hostess asked, pulling an envelope from her purse after giving Lily a thorough visual assessment, her expression turning dismissive.

"Are you kidding?" Lily stammered, shocked.

"You're not an ordinary one, I see. Do you think that nice clothes, bought by my grandson, will hide your intentions? I can spot people like you from a mile away," she said, her eyes appraising Lily. "Now I understand why Laurence didn't like you at first sight. Shall we double it? Or do you want something else? A car? Two cars? A house? A job or your own business abroad?" She glanced nervously over her shoulder. "Make up your mind quickly," she demanded, her stare drilling into Lily.

"I don't want any of this," Lily replied firmly.

"What are you saying? Do you think I can't see past your nice clothes?"

"What are you talking about?"

"The ends of your hair are split in places, your manicure isn't fresh, and your face hasn't seen proper care in a while. Don't take this as an insult, but I can spot flaws even under a ton of makeup, especially if they get in my way," she said, glancing nervously behind her again. "Just understand, you weren't raised like a lady worthy of Dan."

Holy crap, can you imagine that?

"You have an interesting family," said Lily. "The parents have given up on their children, the grandmother is ready to buy her grandson's entire social circle, and the grandson is spending money left and right. I'm not surprised."

"What did you just call me?" the grandmother shouted.

"I'm sorry," Lily said. "I was introduced to you as my boyfriend's grandmother, so I assumed you were her."

"What kind of slum did you grow up in that you don't even know the basic rules of etiquette? You boor!" the grandmother snapped.

"Thank you for your opinion of me, but my family's financial situation is none of your business," Lily replied.

"Oh really?" said the keeper of the house. "Only those who have been taught the rules of handling cutlery, conversational etiquette, perfect waltzing, and other elementary things since childhood will cross the threshold of this house," she said tensely. "And you? Do you think there's a place for you here now?" A victorious smile slowly spread across her face.

"What are you talking about?" Dan asked, out of breath.

"Nothing much," Lily said. "We're just discussing my family's and my financial situation. Nothing new."

"Grandma, you're at it again," Dan said lazily, styling his tousled hair.

"Again? Last time it was at least the daughter of the director of the TIF company, and now? I don't even want to comment on it," she spat, glaring at Lily.

"Then don't. If you're worried about her money or her family, that's my responsibility. Besides, didn't your friend's son have the same situation, and they're happily married?"

"I'm not surprised that Charles's son is capable of that," she said, "but I'm surprised at you! You were taught completely different things since childhood!"

Dan's eyebrow twitched, a sign that his grandmother clearly wasn't an authority figure for him. "You make it sound like I did something illegal," Dan said.

"That's right! You spat on the rules and principles of the family by bringing the first girl you met on the street into this house!" she said.

"Okay, so be it. But do you really think this conversation should be happening in public now? You're being heard all throughout the hall," Dan said, looking defiantly around.

"Are you worried about your reputation? Dan, are you being serious?" his grandmother asked with a bitter smile. "Don't be ridiculous. What reputation are we talking about? You'd think you'd have something left of it. Today everyone saw you with this!" She waved a hand dismissively at Lily. "God, I don't understand what I did wrong to make my grandson stoop so low! I always knew you had terrible taste in girls, and I've long suspected you might do something stupid, but not on a night like this. My dear, I think you can understand something as simple as the fact that you're not wanted here. Laurence will see you out." She directed this last comment at Lily.

"Thank you very much for your kindness, but I'll find my own way out," Lily said firmly, leaving her glass on the nearest table.

"Laurence will help you," the grandmother insisted.

"No, thank you. Have a nice evening," Lily said, as she left the room at a swift pace, her back straight, her face showing no emotions, and her heart still racing inside her chest. She had no desire to hear what Dan had to say to her or argue with his grandmother. It would be pointless and exhausting.

"Wait, I'll come with you!" Dan shouted, catching up to Lily, who was quickening her pace.

"Don't bother," Lily said, taking off her necklace.

"I'll at least take you back home," Dan offered.

"Thank you," Lily said, pressing the necklace into his chest, "for an incredible evening and emotions. By the way, how is Nataly? I think your conversation was fascinating. You came in so out of breath and happy, and also…" She paused, looking him over. "Wipe the lipstick off your neck."

"Wait, Lily, I'll explain everything," he said, grabbing her shoulder.

"Take your hand off me! Have a good evening. I'll send the money for the clothes to your account tomorrow," she shouted back, walking forward.

The street was not too crowded, calm, and slightly cool—an ideal setting for no one to notice the girl who had been walking for an hour, stumbling along the dark road. She was not crying because her heart was broken; she was crying because of the cruelty of people who disregard others' feelings. How many times could Dan have betrayed her? How many times had he and his friends secretly mocked her?

***

If I try to recall my memories from that night, they stop here. The next memory feels like I'm waking up from a long sleep. I'm sitting on a bench, my legs pulled to my stomach, trying to hold them in place with my hands. My stomach hurts as if I was stabbed with a dagger, and with every passing minute, the pain intensifies. I was crying—yes, I was crying, and I'm not ashamed of it. I shouldn't be ashamed now. I cried so hard that, at times, everything seemed to spin before my eyes. Someone asked if I was okay, but I don't remember how the conversation ended.

The second memory is of waking up in the dormitory. Everything in front of my eyes is blurry, but I'm no longer crying; I just want to sleep. A girl is talking to me, her voice familiar and pleasant, but I can't place it…

"Hey! Can you hear me?" someone says from above me.

***

"Emma?"

"Mother of God, did we really get through to her!" Emma exclaims, drawing the others' attention.

"Are you okay?"

"My head is pounding." Lilith tries to put her hand to her throbbing temples, but her hand feels too heavy as if it weren't really hers—like someone had started sewing it on but stopped halfway through.

"I'm glad it's not the alcohol hurting you, but the amount of tears you cried yesterday, broke all records."

"Yes, you couldn't explain anything to us yesterday."

"What time is it?" Lily squints, trying to see outside the window.

"Classes have already started, but we won't let you go without an explanation."

“Say it again, please; I didn’t hear it. It’s too noisy. What’s making the noise? Is it indoors or outdoors?”

“What noise, Lily? The room is quiet.”

The girls exchange puzzled glances.

“I don’t know—here, outside, or in my head, something’s buzzing like crazy. And it’s been flashing in front of my eyes since I woke up.”

“I understand.” Isabelle immediately moved in front of her friend and sat down. “Lily, listen to me carefully. I’m going to ask loudly—what’s written on this sheet?”

“I don’t know; I can’t see. Everything is blurry.” Lily’s hands shook with despair.

“Don’t cry. Let’s try to go to the kitchen. A good breakfast will help—whether it’s a tasty muffin or coffee or tea, it’ll be something,” her friend suggested, trying to help Lily up.

“My legs feel like jelly. It’s hard to get up.”

“It’s okay. You need to eat; it’ll help. Don’t cry.”

Emma encouraged her, and with some effort, Lily managed to get to her feet, the girls helping her slowly move around the room.

“Do you want some tea? Or just a muffin?”

“I don’t know. I don’t want anything…”

“You need to eat something. You’ve had a rough night.”

“I’ll just have tea.”

“Okay, that’s something. Just a minute,” Olivia said as she prepared the tea, and the room fell silent.

“Thank you.”

“Please, Lily, be careful. It’s hot.”

"So, what happened yesterday? Did you and Dan break up?"

"Yeah."

"Why? What did that asshole do?"

"Not now."

"Why?"

"Girls, I feel sick," Lily said, sipping the tea but covering her mouth with her hand.

"What do you mean you feel sick? You've only had half a cup."

"Girls, I'm not joking." She didn't have time to finish as she vomited the tea along with some blood.

"Emma, call 911!"

"Hey, Lily, can you hear me? It's not the best time to sleep."

Chapter 13

The bright light of the lamp cut into my eyes like thin blades. It was cold. Voices echoed from somewhere—screaming and crying—leaving a bitter taste in my mouth. My eyelids were heavy, refusing to lift. Damn it! I couldn't move my arms either. It felt like I was being pulled somewhere, but that lamp kept shining in my eyes. Where am I?

I got my answer in a few seconds as I managed to turn my head to the right. An IV line was connected to my arm. Isabelle was sleeping next to me, and Alex's clothes were on the next bed—he must have gone outside. I twitched my arm slightly, and something beeped, the sound waking Isabelle up. I saw the fear in her eyes as she looked at me.

"Lily, are you okay? How do you feel? Can you talk?"

"Yeah… I'm okay," I wheezed.

"Wait just a minute, I'll be right back. Just don't fall asleep, please."

I nodded weakly as my friend jumped to her feet like she'd been scalded, nearly knocking over a table with medicines on her way out. I covered my eyes. I don't know how much time passed, but she didn't come back alone.

"Darling, this is Dr. Benjamin, the doctor who saved your life. If we'd been just a couple of minutes later, I'm afraid to imagine what could've happened." Isabelle burst into tears as the doctor came closer.

I slowly took the time to look at him.

"Lilith Davis, do you know what condition you were in when you arrived at the hospital?"

"No."

"You don't remember anything at all?" he asked, surprised.

"I just remember my stomach hurting," I said with a sigh.

"Yes, that's part of it. How often did it hurt?"

"Rarely during the day, often in the evening, or when I was nervous."

"Have you had any treatment before?"

"No, although there were some medications I took occasionally to ease the pain."

"So, you were comfortable living with constant pain?" the doctor asked, raising an eyebrow.

"It wasn't fatal."

"I wouldn't say that. You have a gastric ulcer complicated by minor gastrointestinal bleeding. How fatal do you think that is?"

"I'm sorry… what?" I asked, sluggishly.

"You have serious issues, Lilith, that need immediate treatment. You're lucky you got here in time," he said, writing something in his notebook.

"Will I be here long?"

"That depends on how much you want to recover," he said.

I fell silent.

"Lily, I called Alex. He's on his way here. Your brother hasn't left your side for two days. I had to drag him out of here just to get some food."

"Thank you."

No one asked any more questions, and I didn't have the energy for a long conversation. Dr. Benjamin seemed surprisingly nice, but his bluntness was annoying. I understand that, as a doctor, he has to give me a clear diagnosis, but did he have to say, "How fatal do you think that is?" Seriously… handsome, though. I mean, handsome as a man—no more. Dark, neatly styled hair, and light brown eyes that seemed to see right through me. Tall, with an athletic build—he probably has a lot of admirers. Anyway, it's none of my business.

My throat is burning. My whole body is sore. I confirmed my thoughts for another minute or so—my arms and legs were too heavy to lift. It probably wouldn't be an issue if a few strands of hair weren't sitting in my mouth, curled up in the center of my tongue. Although I'm sure the doctors and nurses here have seen more interesting cases. Isabelle left with the doctor, and I started to get annoyed—no, irritated—by how much those few hairs were tickling my nose.

The first attempt to shake out my hair was useless, so I tried shaking my head even harder, as hard as I could at that moment, while simultaneously blowing my nose. Something seemed to start coming out, shifting just a little. And then, of course, Dr. Benjamin walked back in. Do you think that stopped me? No, of course not. By then, I was so irritated that the only thing I could think about was the taste of my hair and the bits that were already in my nose.

Benjamin, like a true gentleman, didn't distract me from my extremely important task for several long minutes. Out of the corner of my eye, I saw him sit down on a chair by the closet, holding some letters in one hand and propping up his cheek with the other. Apparently, he found it interesting to watch a helpless girl fighting her own hair for what felt like a long couple of minutes!

***

"Sorry to interrupt," he said, coughing into his fist.

"No, interrupting what? I'm not doing anything, as you can see. Just solving some things that have irritated me," she said, exhaling again and blowing her nose into her hair.

"And how's that going?" he asked in a serious tone.

"As you can see, the opponent is too potent for me."

"So, I see. And what's your further plan of action?"

"Hmm, let me think—maybe I'll fight to the bitter end," Lily replied, not taking her eyes off her hair.

"I see you're in a good mood, so call me when you win, or when you decide to ask for help."

"Wait!" Lily yelled.

"I'm listening carefully. Did you have something else you wanted to tell me?" He smiled lightly.

"Get him out."

"Get whom out?"

"This long snake that's been lying on my face for an hour."

"Oh, really, you have something like that on your face?"

These were the first words in the whole conversation that fully caught the girl's attention.

"Oh, dear doctor, have you only just noticed? It's a pity, of course, you still look so young, but as they say, age takes its toll."

"I won't argue with that. In any case, it was interesting to watch the performance from the front seat."

"You must be kidding me! What kind of doctor are you to talk to a patient like that?"

"Well, as you can see, that's the kind of doctor I am. You must have been very lucky to end up with me. Okay, joking aside, I still have some work to do. We'll talk about your tests and further treatment later—you're not in a position to focus on serious things right now." Lily burned him with her eyes somewhere in the middle of the sentence, and Benjamin just smiled lightly. "See you later Miss Lilith."

"Wait! Help me get this hay out of my face or you'll be treating my hysteria!"

"So, it's no longer a snake but hay?" Benjamin laughed and came closer. "You're good at threats. I guess your hysteria could be considered a psychological weapon. In that case, I have no choice but to put this hay, that has fallen off the bale, back in."

Benjamin tried his best not to laugh, but the expression on the girl's face thanking him flipped a switch inside him. Puffed-out cheeks and furrowed brows looked at him with a mix of resentment and a drop of anger.

"What now, Lilith? I've already fulfilled your request."

"Does it really look like hay?"

"I don't know; you called it that."

"What do you think it looks like?"

There was a long silence as if they both needed time to think.

"No, it doesn't look like hay at all. I think it looks more like sunbeams or something," he tried to joke, but he was embarrassed by his answer. He quickly stood up and walked to the door. "As I said before, I still have some things to do, so I'll come back later, Lilith."

"Okay."

***

It was silly and nice. Even though Dr. Benjamin seems to be an expert in his field, it also seems that he has no experience talking to women at all.

I don't know what the medical staff and the girls told Alex, but when he burst into the room, he was as pale as the walls of the ward, with sweat running down his forehead. Either he had been running fast, or he was mortally worried about something.

My brother acts like a child every time I'm sick, which is funny because I'm the one who should be acting like a child here, but we've got it reversed. Alex either runs around me every few minutes, offering something to eat or drink, or he sits pale as death, not knowing what to do—and that's normal. He has no experience in caring for someone, considering our father was never too concerned about our health. Despite his constant panic, he does a pretty good job. Although he probably thinks otherwise.

No news from Dan. Although maybe that's for the best. Actually, screw that—it *is* for the best! Bastard! Why invite me along if you already had someone else to go with? Why pretend like we're together? Asshole! I wind through a thousand thoughts in my head, biting my lower lip with all my might. I'm so sick of this. How can I even trust guys when they run after the first short skirt they see?

Oh my God, Lilith, pull yourself together. What did you expect from a guy like that? Did you really think he'd live with you for the rest of your life, have two kids, and build a healthy family? Don't be ridiculous—not with someone like him. He's definitely not made for a serious relationship. God, I hesitated at first, wondering if it was worth it…

Okay, let's summarize: two pieces of news, one good and one bad. The bad news: a guy cheated on me, publicly humiliated me, and, from what I understand, doesn't care at all whether I'm alive now or have already given my soul to God. The good news: the rose-tinted glasses have finally come off my beautiful eyes. I wonder what drug they gave me here that helped clear that filter off? Yeah, everything's fine; everything's great. I'm alone, but I'm strong, and no one will play with me anymore. I'm not a child to go whining.

Damn, it hurts like hell…

In the background, like the TV playing while I was doing my homework, I could hear footsteps in the corridor, the creaking of doors, and the moaning of other patients. For a few seconds, I thought my door was opening, but no one came in.

Chapter 14

I've been working at this clinic for three years now. At first, I was just an intern in training; now, I perform some of the most complicated surgeries and save quite a lot of lives. My colleagues often say that I have a talent, 'hands of gold' or something like that. In any case, I have always loved studying medicine. Since school, biology was the only subject where I wasn't fiddling—I could easily do my best.

As a doctor, I have a good reputation. No patient who was under my care has died, and no surgery I've performed has ended in death…

Neil Ohlar, a patient from ward 108, was admitted to the hospital after a street fight in a barely sober state. Eric Nathan, his fiancée, got into a car accident on the way to meet him. The guy worried so much that due to nervous exhaustion and constant stress, an ulcer opened up. Thank God, he treated it occasionally, so it didn't go too deep.

Lilith Davis, a college student—I can't say she comes from a well-to-do and loving family. But if you look up her medical history, you'll see a rather interesting situation. She has been suffering from chronic gastritis for several years, which later developed into a peptic ulcer. The question arises: why does a girl who doesn't abuse fast food, anything oily, or alcohol have such a condition? It's simple. Some people are like an open book—they cry when they need to, laugh when they're happy, and express anger according to the situation. But there are people like Lilith, who wear a stone mask on the outside while hiding a fragile soul inside. I suspect she held back a lot to avoid showing her vulnerabilities, and it took a hefty toll on her health.

***

"Doctor, it's so good that it's your shift today. Dr. Binley has such a terrible temper—it's not just the patients who are afraid to ask him for help, even the nurses try to stay quiet and avoid catching his eye. By the way, I'm here to ask about our new patients. What should I prepare for tomorrow?" The nurse smiled, her eyes fixed on the doctor, twiddling her fingers nervously.

"The condition of all the new patients is stable. They need rest and, of course, their regular medications. The schedules are next to each of their beds."

"I see, but what about the patients themselves? Is there anything we shouldn't talk about?" The nurse seemed to be searching for something to latch onto.

"I don't know them well enough to answer that. It's better to talk less and keep things professional. That'll help you avoid awkward situations or conflicts."

"Okay, I'll keep that in mind. It's sad how harsh modern life is on today's youth, with so many serious illnesses... Like Henry in Ward 107, whose birthday ended with a trip here. Or Lilith in Ward 110—she's so young and very pretty, isn't she? It's somehow so sad."

"Are you saying that only the old should get sick instead of the young and pretty? I'll say this: when you work in medicine, concepts like justice and emotions take a backseat. Illness can strike anyone, regardless of age, gender, or status. As for whether she's pretty or not, that's an irrelevant question. She's my patient, which means she's equal to everyone else."

"Smart words, maybe I should attend your lectures," the nurse said, clearly impressed.

"No, you shouldn't," he replied, closing the door behind him.

She's just like everyone else; he doesn't single her out. Hurray! Considering that, it means I have a chance; it means he could be mine. Yeah, definitely. Oh, an idea! I'll prepare something for us for lunch. As they say, 'The way to a man's heart is through his stomach.' I had a business card from his favorite restaurant somewhere... Damn it, where did I put it? Oh, found it!

"Yes, hello, I'd like to order a full meal for two."

"Delivery?"

"Yes."

"Okay."

"Payment by card."

"Where to deliver?"

"The hospital, please."

Thirty minutes later, Enith walked gracefully to her doctor's office. "Benjamin, may I come in?" she chirped, opening the door behind her.

"Yes."

"I'm glad you're not busy. I brought some food for us—would you like to have lunch with me?" Without waiting for an answer, she immediately set the table and sat down on a chair opposite Benjamin, or as she called him in her imagination, 'the man of her dreams.'

"Wow, there's so much here. Did you really cook it all yourself?"

"Well, of course I did. Help yourself. Eat, eat," she encouraged, holding out a container of salad.

"I'm pleasantly surprised, Enith. You came in early for your shift, covered for the nurses when needed, and you're always helping me out. I'm sure with such a strong work ethic, you'll go far."

"Really far?" she asked playfully, bursting into laughter.

"I don't know what's in your head, but as for work, I'm sure you'll be noticed by management if you keep this up."

"It's nice to hear that from you." She smiled sweetly, though the charm seemed to have little effect on him.

"Don't worry, anyone could tell you that."

"Not everyone would be happy for me if I got rewarded or given a bonus," she replied, crossing her legs and playfully continuing to chat.

"I agree with you there. Not everyone can genuinely be happy for others, but I believe that kindness and sincerity act like a boomerang."

"That's an interesting theory."

"I have a lot of them," he replied, glancing at a message on his laptop. At that moment, his phone rang, forcing him to interrupt the conversation. "Yes, I'm listening… Of course, I can, but what exactly is the problem? You must be kidding; we just discussed this the other day! Okay, I'll come down now—no, I'll come myself and check everything again."

"I should probably go too," she said quietly, gathering her serving and smiling at the doctor.

"My apologies. As you can see, an emergency."

"I understand."

***

And there are more and more situations like this lately. Now I need to think twice before going on vacation because I'm genuinely worried about the health of the patients and how they'll be treated in the meantime. Moreover, Brian Binley mentioned that he wants to go on vacation too, which means I'll likely be living here for sure.

It may seem like I've put a crown on my head and consider myself better than others. But it's far from that; they're just irresponsible when it comes to important matters and even trivialities. For example, they're sometimes three hours late setting up a drip, or they forget to take it off altogether. Thankfully, it's not as bad as it used to be, but if air really got in during one of those times, what then? Every day, I remind them of their tasks, but as they say, 'in one ear and out the other.' I'm not an exemplary or ideal person who could be called a role model for everyone. No, I'm definitely not. I just try my best to keep everything under control, especially when it comes to patient health.

The only people who consider me a role model are Enith and a few other nurses who are constantly hanging around me. I can guess why, but I'd rather pretend that I'm just not interested. That's right—a grown man, not interested in a relationship. Funny? Maybe. But it's even funnier when my parents remind me every week that they'd already had me at my age, so what's the problem here? I'll tell you what the problem is: I've talked to an extremely large number of girls, both patients and their relatives. The girls were different, and I agree that they were pretty, nice girls, but the problem is that I didn't feel that special spark with any of them. Yes! So laugh if you want—a grown man, looking for a girl with that one small trait that not everyone has. And as of now, I haven't met such a girl yet. Actually, there was one—the sweetest and most special to me. But unfortunately, life is cruel…

Chapter 15

"Honey, how are you?" were the first words Lily heard when she woke up from a deep sleep.

"Everything is fine, Emma, don't worry. The doctors are doing everything they can to help me out, so everything is fine," she said, waving her hand, to which a catheter had been attached just an hour ago.

"I see, girl, but do you know how much you scared us and your brother? Alex and his friends were here last night."

"That's enough!" Isabel snapped. "Can't you see that her room doesn't exactly resemble a fairy tale? Don't make it worse. You want her to blame herself for everything?"

"No, I didn't mean that; I just—"

"We get your 'just'; you're worried. But the only person we can blame with a clean conscience is Dan, right? I think we're all on the same page here."

"Yeah," Lily whispered.

"Has he even contacted you?"

"No, he hasn't."

"That asshole's already started a rumor around the college that he dumped you for cheating," Olivia said.

"Wait, what? Cheating?"

"That's right, what a dick!" Emma puffed out her cheeks.

"I agree, but who else did he involve in this?"

"I don't remember exactly, but he was talking about one of your brother's friends, that you guys had known each other for a long time and you obviously cheated."

"You don't remember the name?" Lily asked, furious.

"Not sure, maybe Leo?"

"He has a boyfriend," Lily answered immediately.

"Gary?"

"He's dating Amy. They're getting married soon."

"Then I don't know for sure." Olivia spread her arms, showing she was at a dead end.

"Okay, I get it. Give me the phone," Lily said insistently, stretching her hand forward and shaking it a little to attract attention.

"Honey, why do you need it?" Emma laughed.

"I want to hear from him personally about who I supposedly cheated on him with," she said and defiantly waved her hand up and down again.

"Are you sure about that? Honey, you can see what he's like—no one has heard from him since you were hospitalized. What a caring guy! He didn't even ask how you're feeling!"

"Isabel, thanks for worrying about me, but I'm fine, seriously. So, give me the damn phone before I rip it to shreds in my mind for the third time."

Someone giggled softly, and her friend handed her the phone. "Thank you." Lily smiled at her.

"Hi Dan, we haven't talked in a while. You won't believe how unexpectedly well things are going for me. I finally got rid of a real jerk. By the way, there's a lovely doctor here who's treating me, and I'm thinking about starting an affair with him. As for why I'm calling, please tell me who exactly I cheated on you with before we broke up. You know, I have so many admirers, and I can't remember everyone who gave me gifts. I felt disgusted then, so I wanted to know who exactly to delete from my phone book. You know, I have the memory of a goldfish—there are just so many people, it's impossible to remember them all. So, will you remind me? It's a shame; he seemed to be a nice person at first, but I don't remember his name."

"I'm glad you're still alive. It's a pity that your common sense left you so quickly," a guy's voice sneered on the other end of the phone.

"What are you talking about, darling? Oh, sorry, habit. No way, are you jealous? Well, I can't help it. Unlike you, I do absolutely nothing to get attention, it just happens. I wonder how?"

"Great acting. I doubt there's a single person who would volunteer to be in a serious relationship with you," he said, laughing into the phone.

"Oh really?" She smiled as she caught Benjamin's eye, waving him over.

He quietly approached.

"Do you mind if I put one of my current admirers on the phone?" she chirped, handing the phone to the doctor.

He stood there for five seconds, recovering from the shock, then picked up the phone and heard Dan's voice say:

"Are you kidding me? Who would look at you unless they were blind?"

"I hate to disappoint you, young man, but I am far from blind and can clearly see the beauty of the girl next to me."

"Who the fuck are you?"

"I'm a man who, unlike you, has spent more time with Lilith in the last few days than you have in your entire relationship."

"Oh, I see. She said something like that. So, you're that doctor? What, do you spoon-feed her too? Change her diapers and bathe her?"

"I think her personal life has nothing to do with you right now, let alone what we're doing together."

Benjamin heard a loud grinding of teeth on the other end of the phone, followed by a loud thump, and then the other person spoke again, "Give her the phone."

Benjamin handed it back to Lily without a word.

"Anything else?" Her eyebrow shot up.

"I just wanted to tell you that I was always sick of you calling me sweetheart or darling or whatever. It was really disgusting to hear those words coming out of your mouth. So, you weren't the only one who had a bad time, dear. You know, it was like a soap opera. Girl, I was just waiting to see when you'd come down from heaven to earth. Do you know how our relationship started? No, not with love—far from it. Although wait, maybe it was out of love, but not for you, for money.

"The day we met, my friends and I bet a lot of money that I could start a relationship with you and keep it going for a while. You know what I mean? All the shopping, meeting my friends who knew nothing about the bet, and the cherry on top was my grandmother. This is your fiasco, girl with a heart of stone or whatever they call you. Night deviless! God! Who gives such nicknames to losers? What do you feel? Pain? Anger? Regret? But who am I asking? Your heart is made of stone.

"And I'm sincerely grateful to you; the only pleasant thing that connects me to you is that thanks to your stupidity, I won a bag of money. No, I'm not a beggar like you, who needs it badly, but I can throw parties at the highest level and have a good time with it if you know what I mean. Well, I've said all I wanted to say. I wish you and your doctor happiness and lots of kids if you haven't already gotten knocked up by someone else."

The room was dead silent as four people waited, anticipating some response from Lily. Dan had hung up, and the unpleasant beeping sound echoed in the room, amplifying the sting of his ugly words. Lily lay there with the phone pressed to her ear for a few more seconds until the screen went dark. First, a single hot tear slid down one cheek, then another followed, and soon they poured down like summer rain—hot, clear drops washing away all the emotions that had come before. She tried to cover them with her hands, to wipe them away, but it was useless.

“I’m sorry… I didn’t know it would be like this. I’m sorry for dragging you into this,” she said, sniffling and confused. “I didn’t realize he was so rotten,” she told Benjamin in a hoarse voice, pausing to wipe her eyes, in which everything was blurry.

“It’s all right, Lilith. You don’t have to worry about that. I take it he was your ex-boyfriend? I think it worked out for the best, considering that you and the guy who doesn’t know basic manners have nothing to do with each other anymore. Isn’t that great?”

“I guess so,” she said, sniffling and staring down at the blanket.

Chapter 16

I left the room. The door closed behind me, and through it, I could still hear the sound of crying—deep, despairing sobs. How do people like that even exist? One thing I can't understand is how someone as incredibly beautiful and open as her could end up with a guy like him. She has that spark, that something special, which means she should have a sea of admirers worthy of her, not some rich boy who thinks the world revolves around his family.

I realized just how angry this situation made me when I found myself spending an hour dwelling on why she didn't leave him sooner, why she believed him, and why she put up with him. My fists kept clenching and unclenching until I finally looked down and noticed what I was doing. All these thoughts were like unsolved puzzles floating in my mind.

I left my office to start my scheduled routine—six patients today, all with the usual: ulcers, gastritis, bile reflux, and some bleeding… When I checked in on the last ward, it was empty of friends or relatives. The girl was curled up on one side of the bed as if trying to protect herself from the world. Her eyes were still wet, with barely noticeable droplets clinging to her eyelashes. I made sure her catheter was secure, checked her general condition, and left. What she needed most now was rest.

The next morning, during my rounds, I noticed that Lily's ward was closed. She was still lying in bed, trying to regain some sense of consciousness, and something told me that no one was coming to see her today. Maybe I was wrong, but usually, by this time, someone was already there. Her ward was supposed to be the first one I opened for visitors. I should just check on her, make sure everything's okay, and move on. But why the hell am I so concerned about her condition after I leave? It's really not my problem—we have a therapist for that.

I went into her ward, and she quickly, subtly wiped her eyes. I pretended not to notice. Everything went according to protocol: temperature, blood pressure, and pulse check. I left her with a few minor instructions, noticing that she didn't really seem to register my presence—her gaze was fixed somewhere distant. But when I asked if she understood everything, she nodded politely. That's it, I can move on.

At least, that's what I told myself, but those empty eyes haunted my thoughts for another half hour. I've always felt sorry for girls in situations like this. I've never tried to justify the 'attraction' of guys who are all hormones and no brains. Girls in these situations are usually more mature, wiser. They feel the weight of responsibility and consequences, unlike guys who change partners like socks and then worry about which one gave them an STD.

I finished checking on all the patients I was responsible for, gave instructions to the nurses, and asked them to let me know when breakfast would be delivered to the wards. Before breakfast time came, I finally had a few minutes to go through the pile of files that had accumulated on my desk—the most important ones being, in my opinion, the medical histories of the new patients. The rest could wait. About twenty minutes later, I was informed that breakfast had been delivered, so I set the files aside again.

***

"Hello, am I interrupting? Can I come in?"

"You're a doctor, and this is your hospital, so you have the right to go wherever you want and whenever you want." Lily smiled wryly.

"You're right, but I do respect my patients' personal boundaries. So, may I come in?"

"Of course," Lily replied.

Benjamin opened his mouth as if to say something else but stopped short. He walked over to Lily's bed and sat on the edge. "How was breakfast?" he asked with genuine curiosity.

"I haven't tried it yet," she answered, maintaining a steady, hard gaze at the doctor's eye level.

"Would you like to try it before it gets cold?"

"Are you trying to pity me?" She smiled tightly.

"And why should I pity you? I have a whole floor full of people like you." He smiled to himself.

"Then why are you making me eat this breakfast?" She raised an eyebrow defiantly.

"It's simple. You're the only kid on the floor refusing to eat the slightly sweetened porridge for breakfast."

"First of all, I'm not a kid, and secondly, I don't like it visually," she replied, and her stomach decided to support her with a loud gurgle.

"Oh really? Okay then, I'll take it away. I think you'll be fine; lunch will be in about six hours," he said, reaching for the plate.

"Hmm..."

"Are you sure?"

There was silence in response. "Okay, I'll give you a few spoons, and then we won't talk about the tasteless porridge again, okay?"

"Are you going to feed me?" she asked in shock.

"Yeah, as you can see. And don't be surprised," he said, pausing for a moment. "So, this is one of the methods of treatment: there's a certain number of spoons of food a person must eat. Ready to start?" he asked seriously, trying to hold back a smile.

Lily looked at him with suspicion for a while, but as the first spoon touched her lips, she opened them to meet it. She savored the porridge in silence while the doctor kept slipping it to her, his eyes fixed on her.

***

Damn, Benjamin, you're a doctor—pull yourself together and take your eyes off her lips for God's sake. But wait, if you do, where will you put the spoon? Never mind! Less staring! Less, I said! Yes, I understand, they're beautiful, pink, plump, and without lipstick, but damn it, you don't have a chance. Remember the rule you made up yourself: 'No matter what, do not get romantic with patients!' All right, exhale slowly. They're not yours. I'm telling you, exhale. It's good that at least the porridge is getting eaten; otherwise, you'd be here until lunch! God, there's a bit of porridge left on her lip... She licked it off with her tongue. *Anyway, my friend, even though we are one and I am the smarter part of you, I'll disappoint you—we're in trouble. I'm also completely lost after this. Well, blink at least once for God's sake!*

Chapter 17

I've been thinking about the plot of my book for an hour now, and I haven't written anything in a long time. So, the main character broke up with her boyfriend, and then what? Will she devote herself to a job? Will she dive into a hobby? Or will she find a new love? Yes, I know the choice is obvious, but what if all her 'friends' are just scum looking for a chance to get a pretty girl into bed? It doesn't matter if they're in a relationship or not. Now she's alone and sad. Sometimes, feelings of anger and despair overwhelm her. She knows that if she ends up in a similar situation again, she'll quit before it reaches the point of no return. As for love, she doesn't see it now, doesn't feel it. The only thing she feels inside is dense darkness, with nothing in it. She doesn't know what love looks like, how it feels, or how to recognize it when it comes. She's just broken into a thousand pieces, trying to put herself back together. There are no words to describe something that's just… not there.

Alex and Dylan are working, and the girls are in college. They wanted to skip classes today, but I assured them I was fine, so they went to college, even though they didn't really want to. So today, the only thing that can entertain me is my book—if you can even call this collection of sentences on my phone a book. The problem is, I can't imagine a happy ending to this story. I don't see the right guy next to her yet. God, why is it so hard? I've been thinking for an hour about the exact moment when he should show up!

And that situation with the porridge—for real? A method of treatment? Yeah, right! He just wanted to make fun of someone, and there I was, lying, exhausted, with a drip in my arm, and he was like, why not? I think that's what happened. But to hell with it—and him too! If he wants to laugh, I'll let him. But the next time they disconnect this drip, it'll be my turn to laugh.

Every day, warm meals are brought to my ward on schedule. For breakfast, it's usually porridge and herbal tea—chamomile or something else. Lunch, in my case, is as light and dietary as possible. And then there are dinners, which have about as many calories as tea. It's funny, but I've been munching on grass like a sheep for a while now. And what's the funniest part? They, those buggers, eat it too and feed it to me! But no, wait! If you look closely, they're stuffing themselves with tons of calories, and they're the ones gaining weight while I'm losing it. Well, that wouldn't be so bad if I actually had something to lose! No, I'm not a model with standard measurements, but I like my chubby thighs and cheeks, so for God's sake, show some mercy and give me something to eat! But it's no use pleading; they don't care anyway. Just like that jerk who somehow ended up on the staff here. Well, what can you do? Things like that happen, I guess…

My grand monologue, performed in duo with all the grace of my emotions, was interrupted by the nurse who brought lunch. I've seen her before, but not often enough to know her name, so I politely thanked her for the food and waited for her to leave. In my mind, I evaluated the weeds with the cauliflower sauce they call lunch here. First things first, I'd already accepted how stupid I must look in her eyes, and the second thing I accepted was that my sweet little tummy wouldn't get anything tasty for another ten or twelve hours.

While I was trying to reason with it, I noticed a cup of tea next to the bowl. Bingo, at least something palatable! I reached for the cup with my free hand, and it was damn hard because the tea was on the nightstand next to my immobilized arm. I made a few more attempts, and the nurse must have noticed my pitiful struggle because she immediately stepped in to stop me.

"You can't move so much; I'll give it to you. Wait," she said, taking the cup in her hands.

I reached out to grab it, but before I could get a good grip, the cup slipped and scalded my hand. It's a good thing it wasn't freshly brewed tea, or my poor hand would've been in serious trouble. I winced as the skin burned and stung. I was wearing a long-sleeved nightgown, so my first instinct was to pull up the sleeve, which now felt like it was melting onto my arm. I placed my aching hand on the arm with the catheter and tried to pull the edge of the sleeve up. My fingers began to burn from the water soaked into my shirt. As I hissed in pain, the nurse, who whispered something like an apology under her breath, barely hiding her wicked amusement, stood by the bedside table with her arms crossed, sneering with a curvy smirk.

***

"Karma's catching up with you," she chirped.

"I'm sorry, what?" Lily said in shock.

"It's not nice to steal a taken man from an almost established family. Oh, not nice at all," she said, shaking her head theatrically.

"What the hell are you talking about? And whatever it is, it certainly doesn't justify your actions!"

"What action, my dear?" Enith asked, her eyes wide with feigned innocence.

"Spilling boiling water on a patient!"

"Oh, how can you say that? I love my job and carry out all my duties with the utmost care. I sincerely don't understand what you're accusing me of," Enith replied, flashing a quick smile before pursing her lips.

"You must not love it that much!"

"What's going on? Is everything okay?" The doctor opened the door to the room.

"Everything is fine, isn't it, Lilith?" Enith said.

Lilith didn't answer. She just pressed her burning hand closer to her body, hoping Benjamin wouldn't notice. But she forgot that the doctor was supposed to examine her regularly and monitor her health. Benjamin approached the bed, and the first thing he noticed was a few drops of tea on the blanket, a mug still lying on the bed, and the hand she was trying so hard to hide.

"Can I see it?" he asked, holding out his hand.

"No, it's okay. I'm fine. I'll call you if I need anything. We agreed on that, didn't we? See, I remember, so you don't have to waste your time worrying about my condition when it's perfectly normal."

He stared at her with a hard, intense gaze for a long moment, then said, "I'll take your word for it, but I still need to examine your arm. You're getting a new drip today, and I need to make sure the nurses can inject it, or I'll have to do it myself. So come on, princess, let me see your hand."

"I'm not a princess," Lily muttered, rolling her eyes.

"And I'm not a prince—but wait. I forgot I was supposed to do this on one knee, right? Just a minute." He stood up and began to dramatically and slowly descend, but Lily stopped him with the very hand he had asked to see.

"Wait. What's this? I had a hunch you were hiding something," he said, glancing at Enith who was shifting from foot to foot, nervously biting her lip. "So, this incident happened with you in the ward? And you just stood there, watching the show from the front row? Really? Get out immediately! In an hour, I'll be waiting for you in my office with an explanation or a letter of resignation. Is that clear?"

Enith just blinked in shock, trying to find a shred of sympathy in the storm of anger radiating from the doctor.

"But I really had nothing to do with it," she hissed, but Lilith shot her a killer look, and Enith quietly walked out.

Benjamin gently pulled Lily's sleeve up to the right height and placed her hand over a bowl of cool water. For fifteen minutes, he poured water over the mild burn, then sprayed it with something and applied an aseptic bandage. He did all this in silence, fully focused on the task.

Lilith could see his long eyelashes, the light stubble that somehow suited him perfectly, and his eyes, deep and inviting like a dense autumn forest. When he bent down, a few stubborn strands of hair fell into his eyes, and at one point, he made an incredible gesture that left Lilith gasping in awe. Benjamin gathered the unruly strands between his fingers and brushed them back as if using a comb, then straightened his back, revealing the muscles that had been hidden until now.

Oh, my God, that's illegal! she thought, blushing and quickly looking away.

"I'm done with your arm. Is there anything else?" he asked, tying off the bandage.

"Huh? No, nothing else," she answered with a confused, shy look.

"Okay, then. Don't get your hand wet, and please don't put any pressure on it like that anymore."

"And what about the drip?"

"I'll have to leave it in this arm for now," Benjamin said, studying her face. "Why are you laughing?"

"Who knows? Maybe it's nervous laughter. Just look how interesting it turned out. First, I couldn't move one arm, but at least I could still do things with the other. And now I'm like a mummy! You forgot to put me in a sarcophagus," she said, wiggling her fingers on both hands and laughing again. "When can the catheter and this bandage be removed?" she asked, looking at him pleadingly, though her eyes still held a glint of anger.

"A few more days, for both."

"Great, and how am I supposed to eat? Change my clothes? Answer the phone? I can't even reach the phone! And what about my book? I'll never finish it!"

"I'll help you," he replied stiffly.

"What?"

"I mean, not with everything, but I think I can handle food, calls, and your book," he said, clearing his throat, then running his eyes over Lily's face, waiting for her reaction, wondering if his offer was appropriate.

"Are you serious? Or are you just trying to make fun of me again?"

"Again? Anyway, I have better things to do than laugh at you." He pouted slightly, and Lily smiled. *Girls can be so unpredictable, and things are rarely as simple as they seem at first glance.* "I'll manage. Besides, I'm not asking you to marry me or anything; I just want to help." He laughed sincerely, and his shoulders, which had been tense as strings a moment ago, slowly relaxed.

"Okay, then I have one more question. Can I rely on you? I mean, you already have a lot of patients, and I might need help at any moment."

"I assure you, I'll come. Maybe not in a second, but fast enough to help you."

"Okay, but why would you do that?" she asked.

He just shrugged. "I don't know."

***

"May I come in?" Enith asked timidly.

"Yes, of course. I've been waiting for you for fifteen minutes," he replied, holding his face in his hand.

"Benjamin, you're not serious, right? I've worked here for six years. The team has become like family, and so have you…"

"It's not obvious, considering how you're betraying your own team. But I have a question: were you thinking about anything at that moment?" he asked, raising an eyebrow as if genuinely curious.

"Have you ever heard about girls being jealous?" she said through gritted teeth, her gaze shifting unsteadily between him and the table.

"What are you talking about?"

"I'm sure everyone has noticed how much you like your new patient. I agree she's pretty, but she's not your type, right? You seem blind," she said, walking around the table and stopping behind him. "I was here all along, I was giving you hints," she murmured, wrapping her arms around him from behind. "But I didn't expect this. I was the one who was here all this time, not that wench. You don't even know her! God, who am I talking to? You're not listening to me now. She's in your head again, isn't she? You'll make me laugh if you tell me it's just my imagination. Go ahead and tell everyone I made it all up! Convince everyone you have no feelings for her. I'm here every day, giving it my all: clothes, makeup, hair, food. What the hell is wrong with me, huh?"

“Is that everything you had to say?” he replied in a flat tone, shuffling through the papers on the table.

“No, not everything! I want to hear how she’s better than me.”

“I don’t know what she’s capable of, but I’m pretty sure she wouldn’t have poured scalding hot tea on someone on a whim. How about that?”

“So, you do like her, after all?” she said, narrowing her eyes.

“That’s none of your business,” he replied, still calm.

“You’ve got to be kidding me! Can you give me a clear answer: are we going to be together or not?”

“Enith, I have a question: have I ever given you any reason to think about our relationship in that way? Have I ever shown any gesture of sympathy? Have I made any suggestion that goes beyond work? And I’ll ask you not to rely on your imagination now; it’s already gotten you into this mess.”

“You know, it’s cruel.”

“Is it cruel not to return affection when you don’t feel the same way?”

“That too. But it’s even crueler to flirt with someone else right in front of me.”

“That’s enough, Enith,” he said, handing her a pen and a blank sheet of paper. “I’ll submit your resignation to HR myself.”

Chapter 18

Enith walked out, and I felt the heavy burden I had been carrying finally collapse to the floor, spilling everything that had been weighing me down. It was a strange feeling, really strange. At first, you get used to it, turning a blind eye to most things, but we can't always stay blind, can we?

As Lilith and I agreed earlier, I will help her. While making my rounds on the floor, I was informed that her brother, along with his boyfriend and a friend, had just visited her. Whether it was the brother's friend or Lilith's, the nurse could not tell, so I decided to take my time and let them have their visit. After all, I think her brother wouldn't be too thrilled to see a doctor spoon-feeding a patient or typing on her phone while she dictates to him.

***

"Lily, what happened?" Alex looked at my hand.

"An accident," I said, trying to smile, though it probably came out wrong.

"I mean, how could this happen in a hospital? Where are the staff? Where's the doctor who's responsible for you?"

I could tell that if Dylan wasn't holding my brother back, Alex would have already stormed into the corridor to have a different kind of conversation with Benjamin.

"Alex, the doctor had nothing to do with this." I exhaled heavily.

"And since when is a doctor not responsible for patient injuries in their ward?"

"Alex, calm down. It's really not his fault, and the nurse who did it has already been fired."

"Is he young?" Dylan asked, changing the subject.

"Yeah."

"Handsome?"

"Yes." Of course at this moment, I rolled my eyes.

"Alex, dear, maybe you haven't realized it yet, but we have two problems. The first is her arm, which seems to be starting to heal." He ran a nervous hand through his hair as he continued, "The second is the young and handsome doctor she's defending. Have you ever talked to him?"

"No, but I see that I should."

"You shouldn't!"

"Lily, dear, the most important thing for you now is to stay calm and recover quickly, while the men are going to have a small talk."

"And what are you going to talk about?"

"About how tender and good you are, and that we won't let any random guy take you."

"What? Dylan, say something to him, because if I could move my hands, I would smack him for this." I looked for help in Dylan's eyes, nervously clenching my fingers.

"You're such a meanie. Why, I agree with him. You've grown up to be a real beauty, Lily. And as your brother said, we won't let any random guy take you." Dylan laughed kindly, while I panicked.

Are they really going to tell him all this bullshit and then go home with a clean conscience, leaving me to clean up the mess? No, I'm not taking part in this.

"Don't worry, girl, I'll keep an eye on them just in case. We'll be in touch." Mary winked at me, and I wiggled my right index finger in response, "Yeah, in touch."

***

Dr. Benjamin had just walked into his office and closed the door behind him when he heard a loud knock.

"Come in."

"Thank you for the invitation," Alex said, closing the door behind him and Dylan. They probably decided not to involve Mary in a purely manly conversation.

"Damn, Dylan, he's really cute and probably young if my eyes are still working properly."

***

I laughed slightly as I watched the scene unfold in my office. "I'm sorry to interrupt. I'm pleased to hear that I'm good-looking, and yes, I'm still young, only twenty-three. But what's the reason you came in?"

My words hung in the air for a long minute. No one said a word. The two guys stared at me and seemed to communicate without words.

"He's too old for her!" Alex hissed.

"I think he's just right, and he's a doctor, which means he's ready to start a family," Dylan said, turning to Alex with a challenging look.

"Are you crazy? What family? I haven't even agreed to a relationship yet."

"Hey, I'm just thinking about the future," Dylan said, barely containing his laughter.

"Do you have a girlfriend?"

"No."

"Do you live alone or with your parents?"

"Alone."

"Does your job pay you more than… thousands a month?"

"Yes."

"Hmm, do you have serious intentions toward my sister?" These words hit me like lightning.

"What?"

"Well, maybe it's a little unexpected, but I'm the only family she has left, so I have to make sure," he said. "Lily recently broke up with some jerk whose ass I haven't had a chance to kick yet. I think you know about her previous relationship, right? I just want to make sure she'll be safe with you."

I stood there, listening to this performance as if there were another doctor behind me they were referring to. "Uhm, yes, I heard about her story, and I'm very sorry. I'd like to apologize for the tea incident. The nurse responsible for serving breakfast in the morning has already been fired. I change Lily's bandages every few hours, and we agreed that I would help with food, calls, and writing the book."

I saw them studying me. Her brother was still raising his eyebrows, and the guy next to him shook his head in approval.

"Can you give more details about the book?"

"I don't know much yet. I'll probably be helping her to write it one of these days. If you have any questions about it then, I'll answer them," I finished, standing with my hands on my sides.

"Okay."

"You seem like a good guy, doctor. I think I don't have to worry about Lily," the guy who came with Lily's brother said, smiling at me.

"You can call me Benjamin. You're not my patients, and we're almost the same age anyway."

"Okay, then you're probably wondering, and I'll answer: he's my boyfriend," Dylan pointed at Alex. "We've been raising Lily together since she was a little kid, so she's like a little treasure for us. Someone tried to steal her once, but this time we'll stay in touch with her more so we can be at the right place at the right time."

"Thank you for telling me all this." I blinked in confusion.

"So, what are your intentions?"

I had just managed to exhale with relief, but it was too soon.

"Yes, she's pretty, but I'm not thinking about—" I began, but Dylan interrupted.

"We've understood everything. You're a doctor, anyway. You know the consequences and what's what. I think we can end this conversation," Dylan said, pushing Alex toward the door. But he stopped with his hand on my shoulder. "I trust you, man. She really deserves the best, and it's not just because she's ours."

I gave them a look, waited for the door to close, and collapsed into a chair. What had just happened? Was this like meeting the bride's family without knowing the bride herself? I came to my senses as soon as I realized that if someone opened the door and saw me, red as a tomato, with a smile on my face, they'd probably think: *He's gone insane.* Maybe I am. I just fired Enith, who had worked here for a long time and was flirting with me, who maybe one day would have got what she wanted. But now I was happy that the brother of a pretty girl gave me the go-ahead for a relationship. Really? I slapped my face with my palms, a good way to come to my senses.

***

When I went to Lily's ward, I noticed that the food had been sitting on the table by her bed for some time. Her friend must have helped her change her clothes during the visit. I walked over to the table, took the now slightly cooled food, and sat down on the edge of her bed.

"Why didn't you eat?" I asked, scooping up a spoonful of mashed potatoes and bringing it to her mouth.

"Uhm… I was waiting for you." She tried to sound serious but immediately broke into laughter.

"I'm sorry for the delay. I was talking to your brother," I said, taking another spoonful of mashed potatoes.

"What did he want?"

"Nothing much, just a man-to-man conversation," I replied, the edge of my lips lifting into a smile.

"Is that so?"

"Doesn't the young lady trust her brother?"

"No, on the contrary, I know exactly what to expect from him," she said, her cheeks rapidly turning pink.

"And why is that?" I asked, trying to play innocent.

"Hmm… My brother is very meticulous about choosing a good boyfriend for me…" She paused, glancing at me with a shy smile. "And you must have passed all his criteria."

"Really?" I asked, my grin widening. "Don't turn your head away; there are still a few more spoons left."

"I can't; it's too much," she said frowning.

"I believe you, but you've lost a lot of weight, so we need to fix that. By the way, what are your plans for the evening?"

"I would like to write at least a few lines for my book…"

"A book, you say…"

"You won't be able to do it?"

"Why not? I'll be free in about two hours. If you don't mind, we can start writing then, okay?"

"Okay." She smiled slightly.

***

After the doctor left, I felt my stomach pushing me into the bed; the portion was really too big! I told him I couldn't eat that much! But I ate it anyway… How did he manage to stuff all that into me? Of course, he did it while talking and smiling, distracting me with his eyes, his lips stretching into that charming smile, and his perfectly ironed white robe. He fed me spoon after spoon! What a sneaky guy!

As he said, exactly two hours later, the door to the ward opened, and he quietly entered. It was already dark outside; eight in the evening felt like two in the morning. The ward was quiet, dark, and cold. Patients were going about their business in their rooms, with noisy phone conversations drifting from next door through the barely open crack of the door. The girl from the first ward usually read her books at this time, and the guy from the opposite room was engrossed in some game with a weird ball on the screen.

He pulled a chair over to my bed, sat down with his robe open, and asked, "What should I do?"

Chapter 19

I was sitting on a chair, holding the girl's phone. I was overwhelmed with unusual emotions; it was something new and interesting. "Can you tell me in a nutshell what the book is about?" I asked.

"Is it necessary?" She exhaled tiredly.

"No, probably not. I was just wondering what genre I'll be writing in now."

She frowned. "It's a novel, and the girl has just broken up with her boyfriend."

"I see," I muttered thoughtfully.

"So, uhm… shall we get started?"

"I'm ready. Where do we start?"

"Will you read the last sentence so that I can get my bearings?" She looked at me expectantly.

I scrolled through the book to the very end. There it was: "How can I write about love and pour all its colors on paper when I've never seen them myself? It's strange, isn't it? The only colors I've ever seen were red at first, and somehow, in a mixture of emotions, they turned dark and swampy green. It's hard… Something inside me is broken, and something tells me it will take a long time to mend it…"

I cleared my throat as I finished reading the paragraph, and Lily finally focused her gaze on me.

"So, shall we get started?"

"Yeah… Where would you start?"

"It's hard to say. I don't know where she is or who she's with. The only thing I could feel was her state of mind. I would probably start with a new chapter in the book."

"Let's try," she said uncertainly, and I noticed she was trying her best not to meet my eyes.

"Okay, right. Chapter twenty-three—what should we write?"

"Nowadays everyone has the opportunity to be reborn like a phoenix. A broken heart cannot be glued back together, but there is better medicine than glue, and everyone will meet it," she reflected, and I wrote.

"Got it."

"Yes, this situation knocked me out. It left its wounds and drops of poison that are still being washed out from my body. But I decided that this will not happen again. I will not be a sincere and open book for those who do not deserve it! I will be strong! I will set a goal for myself; boys are not the main thing in life. And yes, it's not a tantrum now, in case you're wondering. I just try not to obsess about such things. I want to finish the book, publish it in a good publishing house, and make my future and the future of my parents better."

She finished speaking, and I wrote down the last few words. While writing, I was tormented by the question: were these really the words of the character from the book, or was she just pouring out her soul? The main character is too much like her, and this situation with the boyfriend is too similar, but I am glad that she wants to be strong. She will be strong; she has a goal, and she's going for it.

"Is that all?"

"That's all for today. Thank you." She smiled slightly, darting her eyes again. "You were a big help to me."

"I'm glad to help. Tomorrow at this time again?"

"Is it possible?" I noticed her eyes sparkled.

"Yes, young lady, it is possible."

"Great, I look forward to tomorrow."

"No one's ever said that about my visits to their ward."

"You're such a joker. Get used to it."

***

The next day, Dr. Benjamin arrived at the promised time. Alex was sitting in Lily's ward, and Dylan had stepped into the corridor to take a phone call.

"Hello, here for a routine checkup?" Alex smiled at him thoughtfully.

"Not exactly. Lily asked me to help her with something, so we agreed I'd come by now."

"So, princess, this is why you tried so hard to get us out of here? It's all about him?" Alex said, gathering his things. "Good luck with your plans," he added with a wink to Benjamin.

"Alex!" Lily called out, but he had already closed the door behind him. "Don't take it personally; he's not usually like this... well, sometimes, but I really don't know what that was about."

"It's okay. He was the same when he came into my office," Benjamin said with a slight smile. "So, what are your plans for the book's plot?"

"I'm not sure. I've been thinking about it for a while, but no matter how hard I try, I can't figure out how to fit another guy into the story. What will he be like? How will they meet? How do I describe love…?" She whispered the last words almost inaudibly.

"Well, let's see," the doctor said, slapping his hands on his knees. "Where is she now, and who is with her?"

"She's at home, has been staying in her room for a while now, skipping college."

"Did anyone at college like her?"

"No."

"Then I have a perfect idea," he said with a clever smile, gazing ahead as if envisioning an invisible scene.

"Really?" Lily raised an eyebrow in disbelief, ready to listen.

"Yeah. Here's my idea: your main character finally leaves home and goes to college—"

"And on her way, she gets hit by a car, and the driver turns out to be her destiny?" Lily interrupted.

"Not exactly, though I did consider that idea," he continued, and Lily lightly rolled her eyes. "So, she goes to college, and literally the next day, a young, handsome, muscular guy with a good sense of humor starts working as a teacher. Of course, no one will cling to him intentionally, it'll all happen naturally. What do you think?" Benjamin waited eagerly for praise, like a puppy seeking approval.

"It will be hard to describe," she said, biting her lip.

"I wouldn't say that," he replied, gently wiping her lip with a napkin. "You're biting it until it bleeds. What should I do with you?"

"Can you describe this?" she asked.

"I think so."

"I'm surprised you haven't published any books yourself yet. You're really talented at this."

"I'm starting to worry about it too. I didn't expect this from myself." He smiled at Lily and continued. "So, 'Today is the first time I've left the house in a long time…'?"

Lily nodded in approval.

Chapter 20

I was lying on the bed, staring at the ceiling. For fifteen minutes, my eyes were fixed on a family of spiders planning to cross the vast white field of the ceiling above me. The nurse had told me I'd be stuck here for two more weeks. A long couple of weeks.

My brother asked me about the book. I don't know how he even knew about it, but I had nowhere to go and had to tell him. In the end, he was pleased, saying he liked everything about it, though I should work on my grammar. Then he said something like this:

"Society will always put pressure on you; competition has existed since the beginning of time. If you succeed, people will be jealous. If you fail, they'll be happy they're better than you. So don't give up—you're strong, Lily." He kissed me on the forehead and said goodbye, and I thought about his words for a while. I wondered if he really believed I'd be able to publish it someday.

Benjamin had said something similar: "If you're trying to write a book and get closer to your goal but fail, congratulations—you're moving forward. Most people don't even try. It's usually much easier to just comment on other people's failures than to try to step into their shoes."

When I asked him, "What if I reach out to ten publishers and they all reject me?"

"You'll gain invaluable experience," he replied.

"That experience would be useless. The book won't be published, I won't get paid, and I'll just regret the time wasted."

"If you're only in it for the money, I advise you to give up right now. Books like that usually lack emotion or soul, and in the struggle for large circulation, authors forget what it means to truly be an author."

"I'm not chasing money!" I insisted.

"Okay, that's great. Then what do you want from your books?"

"I want my books to reach the people who need them. I want them to see what's inside, to look at situations from both the viewer's and the protagonist's point of view. Books are my safe future, even if it's only a small amount of money. Eventually, there will be a time when I'll need it."

Benjamin just smiled and nodded in approval, and that was the end of our conversation.

***

Christmas holidays are my favorite, and I usually celebrate them with Dylan and Alex at their house. There's magic in the air, and all the houses are decorated like little gingerbread houses—like the ones everyone probably made with their parents as kids. At the start of the month, people search through most of the shops in the city to find the best gifts for their loved ones. Children make Christmas decorations for the house and the Christmas tree. We've never had a live tree for Christmas; it's almost a tradition now to use old artificial ones. Both ours and Dylan's tree are about the same age as me.

Now, I dreaded the thought of everything I'd miss. The presents, for sure… I wouldn't be able to shop for anything for at least another week. I furrowed my eyebrows and waited for the doctor to arrive. We were going to have a serious conversation! We'll play a little chess game!

When the doctor entered the room, I immediately made my move.

Скоро Різдво знаєте я так обожнюю це свято

"Christmas is coming soon, you know I love this holiday so much," I said.

"Me too," he replied, sitting down on the edge of the bed. His pawn stepped forward on the other side of the board.

"I'm looking forward to decorating the house and the tree," I continued as he connected the catheter.

"I understand. I also love these days—everything just shines with its charm," he said, thinking over his words.

"That's exactly what I mean." I moved another pawn forward. "I'm telling myself that in another week, I'll be out of here and into the hustle and bustle of preparing for the holidays. Isn't that great?" I chirped, waiting for his move.

"Of course. You'll still have time to prepare, buy gifts, and all that, but you won't be out of here for another week and a half. Remember what I said?" He smiled at me, and meanwhile, I saw one of my pawns disappear from the board. I bit my lip; the game wasn't over yet.

"Oh really? That's strange; it somehow completely slipped my mind. I've been feeling great lately; maybe that's why I forgot," I said, trying to catch him off guard. *What do you say to that, huh?*

"Oh, that's great. Then you'll have enough time to write your book in peace. Isn't that good?" The corner of his mouth turned up, and I could see myself in his eyes. They clearly said, 'One more pawn down.'

"I'm sure it's great, but I think I'd be better off at home with Alex," I said, giving him one of my most attractive and convincing smiles from my arsenal.

"As for Alex, he's all for you staying in the hospital as long as it takes. He completely trusts me to make the call."

The IV started slowly dripping into my veins, and I felt drowsy, but in my head, I was thinking, *One more down.* "You're strange. Do you really want to be here for the holidays? Why do you need another patient? You could just send me home to get better and, meanwhile, like all normal people, spend your saved time preparing for the holidays."

"I can't," he answered painfully.

"And why's that? What's the problem?"

"Unlike you, I'm kept here by a promise I once made to a girl," he said, his voice growing quieter. "She's gone… and I cannot break my promise."

"Was she dear to you?" I crumpled on the bed, realizing how close I was to crossing a line. What started as a childish game of chess had turned into something much deeper.

"Yes, very."

"W-wanna talk about it?" I dared to ask, catching his eyes, which were fixed on his hands.

"I think now's not the best time for such talks, Lilith. You have enough problems of your own, and for health reasons, you're not allowed to worry. As a doctor, I can't let that happen."

"You know, it's a little more complicated than that. I'm going to worry anyway; the only question is how much. That depends on you," I said with a wry smile, and he understood what I meant.

Exhaling heavily, Benjamin sat down next to me again. "Don't pity me, and don't make that expression on your face from now on," he said, nodding at me, though I was sure he was looking at the bed.

"We dated six years ago when I was only a sophomore. She was my childhood friend, so even before our relationship, she was close to me. The situation that turned my life around happened on the day we had a date planned. I waited for her at the meeting place for a long time until I got a call from the city hospital: 'Are you Emma Laurent's boyfriend?' I answered something unintelligible, and they continued, 'My condolences. At sixteen ten local time, Emma passed away. The doctors did everything they could, but the injuries were too severe.' I tried to process what they were saying, but the words didn't stick together. When I finally realized that Emma was dead, I was broken…" He stopped, breathing heavily.

I knew what he was feeling. Maybe my experience was lighter, but I knew what it was like. Without even realizing it, I put my hand over his, and he jumped as if waking from a nightmare, quickly regaining control.

"When I finally pulled myself together, I remembered the promise we made to each other long before we entered university. That's why I'm here now. And no, Lilith, I'm not going to let you go any sooner just because the painkillers are working well."

I smiled at him but didn't remove my hand from his. For a few minutes, he told me about what had almost broken him, but then he returned to being the doctor I knew: persistent, with a movie-star smile and some other trait that touched me.

Chapter 21

I almost let my guard down in front of Lilith. A year or two ago, a conversation like that would have easily thrown me off track, but now I'm okay. Over time, we adapt. Well, maybe it's more accurate to say that over time, we come to terms with the situation. We accept the facts and get used to the life we have now.

I used to catch myself thinking about what could have happened if I had gone to meet her. What if I had met her at her house? What if we had made plans for another day or for a different time? These questions tore me up inside because I knew, or at least I wanted to believe, that I could have done something. But it was just my thoughts—thoughts that tormented me in my dreams for many years. There were nights when I woke up in a cold sweat, screaming her name, or crying out, "Why her?"

As strange as it may seem, when you really hammer something into your head, it works. You can convince yourself that the past should stay in the past because there's still a whole life ahead. It works the same way as when you tell yourself not to regret the past, justifying it by saying that you can't change anything and that in the future, you'll have many more opportunities to do things differently, maybe even under better circumstances.

Over the years, I've come to the conclusion that a person truly comes to terms with the loss of someone when they can talk about it freely.

Swallowing all the words about Emma, I looked at the hand that had been gently stroking mine the entire time. It was such a small gesture, one that could have easily gone unnoticed, but it was so comforting and warm.

***

"Okay, let's see… Raven rushes into the history classroom like a gust of fresh wind. There were no students there yet, so she had time to run through the topic assigned for today's class. Rumor had it that the history teacher, who had been here last week, snapped and quit. According to him, their group drove him to it, so now everyone was eagerly waiting for the next 'victim.'

"Raven leaned over her notebook, thinking carefully, and didn't notice that she was no longer alone in the classroom. A sharp knock, as if something had fallen, brought her back to her senses. She jumped up and looked around for the source of the noise. 'I knew I was clumsy, but not to that extent,' the man muttered quietly under his breath as he leaned over a pile of papers that had scattered across the room.

"'Here, is this yours?' Raven asked, picking up the papers that had flown in her direction.

"'Yes, thank you.' He nodded slightly and continued gathering the papers, never looking up. From the back, it was hard to see who he was. The man wore a stylish shirt tucked into his pants, had slightly disheveled dark hair, and Raven caught a glimpse of glasses before he turned his back to her. She quickly joined him and began collecting the papers—one sheet, another, and another, until they accidentally tugged on the last one at the same time.

"'Oh, sorry, it's yours,' she said, embarrassed.

"It's okay, thanks for your help," he replied calmly, starting to get up.

"'Still, I'm sorry for the…' She didn't have time to finish as her jaw dropped in shock. *Oh my God, is this a joke?* In front of Raven stood a handsome young man. His glasses, which are usually hard to pick, completed his already perfect look, and beneath his shirt, his muscles shone. If anyone says Apollo doesn't exist, they should definitely look at this guy.

"Did I write it right?" Benjamin asked smiling, his eyes radiating. "Praise me; didn't I do a good job?"

"Everything is great, but their meeting reminds me of some sort of fairy tale," Lily replied.

"And what's wrong with fairy tales? The prince finds his princess, and everything is great."

"You know that this rarely happens in real life—almost never. There are always problems, difficulties, and stuff like that."

"Difficulties, you say?" He pondered. "Let's say, for realism's sake, he, as a teacher, is strictly forbidden to date students, risking his job and reputation."

"You're right…"

"And isn't that a difficulty for you, and not just an imaginary one?"

"Uh-huh," Lily considered the doctor's words.

He continued, "Do you want me to describe him in more detail?" He waggled his eyebrows.

"Oh, you've really gotten carried away. I must ask, is he your type or what?" Lily laughed.

"Interesting question. I think if I were a girl, I would immediately sit down to write a plan of action to win over such a guy," he said, proudly raising his head.

"And in reality, are there many girls trying to win you over?"

"Quite a few," he answered, turning his gaze to Lily. "Why do you ask?"

"Uh, just wondering," she replied. The moment their gazes met, she quickly shifted her eyes to her hands, the bed, and the door, unable to keep them in one place. Something inside her fought to look at Benjamin.

"Are you sure?" he asked, his eyes still on her.

Lily was incredibly embarrassed. In a few minutes, her ears and cheeks turned as red as if they were painted, and Benjamin's eyes certainly noticed.

"Okay, just wondering then." He theatrically sighed and returned to the book.

Lily secretly watched him, her thick eyebrows and plump lips making her want to look at him more. Her hand seemed to have a mind of its own, longing to touch the soft, probably tousled hair that fell into Ben's eyes. His hands were twice as big as hers—manly, handsome… On that note, she saw the corner of his mouth turn up. *Damn it!* He'd seen her looking at him!

"Why are you smiling?" she snapped.

"I must be your type if you're looking at me like that."

"Dream on."

"I will!"

"Good luck."

"Thank you."

"Wait, are you saying that *I'm* your type?" Lily asked, her eyes widening in shock.

Benjamin, realizing the conversation would be a long one, set his laptop aside and smiled. "Let's say that's the case."

"And why is that?" Lily asked seriously, curling her fingers. "Is it because of the looks? No, that can't be it. I look terrible right now. Sense of humor? Oh God, what am I even thinking about? Well, I'm not really that interesting, but Emma and Olivia, for example, are. I'm surprised you haven't fallen for their charms yet."

"Maybe they're not as strong as yours."

"Enough of these jokes. I'm serious." For the first time, Lily looked confidently into his eyes, but he didn't move.

"Me too," he said, a wry smile crossing his face. "I know I'm hopeless and have no chance, but since we're on the subject, I decided to take advantage of the opportunity I have. Maybe it's just a little sympathy that you won't believe. You know, I probably felt the despair of people who never say what they feel. You won't be here soon, and I'll be left alone with these feelings. Now I won't regret not saying anything. It's a little selfish on my part, so sorry for that."

"You're kidding, right?" She looked into his eyes, then down at her hands, already sweating noticeably.

"My father once told me that it's a person's way of thinking that will raise your future children, not a pretty face or looks."

"Is this a hint that I'm not beautiful?"

Lily received only a heavy look in response.

"Okay, bad joke."

"You are extremely beautiful, and it scares me." He exhaled heavily again; this time it wasn't acting.

"Why?"

"I can't control myself." He clenched his fist slightly and looked away.

"Control?" Lily asked, as if the answer wasn't obvious. She continued to look at his face, her lips moving as the words came out.

"You probably won't like what I want to do," Benjamin said.

Lily swallowed hard, her hands sweating, her cheeks burning as if she were a foot from a flame. But she still said, "And how will you know if you don't try?"

For the first time in the last few minutes, he looked from the bed to her eyes, then to her plump, red lips, which she was nervously biting. Ben muttered something under his breath and gently placed his hand on her cheek. She froze, her teeth releasing her lower lip, making it even more plump. At first, he gently ran his palm over her cheek, keeping eye contact with her. Then his hand dropped, his thumb tracing over her lower lip, still stinging from the long bite.

"I told you not to do that." His eyes were fixed on her lips, and his finger traced their curves. His other hand covered Lilith's hand, and she went limp. It was as if he was waiting for permission to proceed, and Lily gave him a confident look, convincing him to move on.

Benjamin didn't think twice. He covered her lips with his own, and everything around him seemed to freeze. He tasted her red, plump lips—they were as soft as he had imagined. Lily looked into his eyes in confusion. A few seconds ago, she had a bundle of confidence that would have moved mountains, but now, just the touch of his lips brought her out of the game. He made eye contact with her again, ran his hand, which had been exploring her lips, through her hair, and kissed her again.

Lily closed her eyes. It wasn't her first kiss, but it felt like her first, and she had never experienced such sensations during a kiss before. Her heart leaped to her head, trying to respond in kind, then fell to her feet, realizing what was happening. His hand gently stroked her hair, and his lips passionately and gently covered hers, as if they were in another universe… Until a shout rang out in the corridor:

"Doctor! There's a critical situation in ward ten!"

He jumped to his feet as if scalded, picking up the sheets and his laptop.

"I'm sorry, I shouldn't have done that," was the last thing he said that day, without hearing Lily's response.

Chapter 22

Goddamn, who does it like that? First, he kisses you, then hides like a kindergartener! He didn't even give me a chance to respond, and then people say that women are the ones who make things up, create problems, and get offended over nothing! He was supposed to come by at six, and I knew it perfectly well. If there were times he could swap his duties with a nurse, those moments are over now—he can't avoid the conversation any longer.

He must have no idea of how hard it was for me to stay calm yesterday when I was talking to my brother, especially with Dylan there. The difficulty doubled. My brother takes everything too seriously, and Dylan, unlike him, had long ago asked if I had a boyfriend or if I liked someone. I kept most of what happened between Dan and me under wraps, but in the hospital, when both of them looked at me with that caring expression that only the closest people give you, we talked in more detail. At first, Alex wanted to cut Dan into pieces and roll him into the asphalt, but Dylan stopped him right away, saying that we needed to come up with something less illegal. And that's how our conversation about Dan ended.

As for Benjamin, I think Dylan tried to bring it up, but I just shrugged it off, wondering why I should even talk about it. I wish I could've heard my brother's and Dylan's opinions on what Benjamin is really like. I bet it would be an interesting lecture, and I should try to get them to spill the tea somehow. After their conversation with Benjamin, they seemed very friendly with him, as if they'd known each other for at least five years and Alex gave his blessing for our wedding four of those five years ago. They're definitely hiding something…

I waited for six o'clock like a child waiting for a Christmas present, and it finally came. Benjamin acted normal and did his job perfectly. Everything was great except for one thing: he didn't say a word about what happened yesterday, and his eyes never met mine the entire time he was in my room.

Just as he was about to leave my bedside, I grabbed him by the sleeve. "Please stay; we need to talk," I said. He swallowed visibly, and I added, "It won't take long."

"Okay," he replied, sitting timidly on the edge of the bed, looking at me with a sad expression, as if he already knew what the conversation was about and had braced himself for the worst possible outcome.

"Yesterday, you were braver," I teased.

"Yesterday, adrenaline was raging in my veins," he said, his gaze shifting between my face and the bed, never settling in one place for long.

"And what caused that?" I asked, trying to push him to a different course of action.

"You."

"Okay, then why have you been avoiding me all day?"

"Even though I'm an adult, you can laugh, but this is my first real relationship," he said, wrapping a strand of my hair around his finger. I felt breathless. "I mean, my first real kiss as an adult, and I'm not sure it was perfect. I'm not even sure you wanted it," he added, shrugging nervously.

"Seriously? You've been getting on my nerves all day because of that stupid thing?"

"Well, you're right; it's stupid," he admitted, nervously clenching his fist. "So, what did you want to say?"

"I didn't give you an answer yesterday," I began, noticing him swallow hard again. "You know, you're a cool doctor, a handsome guy, and like you said, you have 'quite a few' admirers." His gaze silently devoured me as I looked away. "I liked our kiss. I still remember the touch of your hand in my hair, and I think I like you."

I heard a heavy, long exhale followed by another gulp. I didn't dare look him in the eye, but I knew he was staring right at me.

"My heart is pounding like it's ready to jump out," he muttered under his breath.

"Should I call a doctor?" I joked, jumping up and looking toward the door.

"My doctor is already here," he said with a shy smile, as if he couldn't believe it, holding my hand in his and kissing it gently, almost imperceptibly. I stood there looking at his face, and this time, I found something new, something I hadn't seen before.

***

There are still four days until I get out of the hospital, and Benjamin has also realized how difficult it will be to adjust to seeing me only once or twice a week. My hand, which had a slight burn, has long since healed, and I can finally do basic things on my own. But Benjamin insists on continuing to help me with everything until I leave, regardless of whether I have one or both hands working. So, my morning began with delicious porridge, which he gently fed me spoonful by spoonful, and ended with me working on my book. He was right: the love affair between a teacher and a student isn't as easy as it seems, but it's definitely intriguing!

For several days now, I've been wondering how to tell my brother about this ridiculous situation. Does this mean I'm in a relationship now? Wait, really? Oh my God, I'm in a relationship with a real Apollo, and I'm still worried about what my brother will say?

***

"Hi. Can't reach Alex. I'd like to talk to you."

"Hi, Lily. Alex went to the shop. Is something wrong? Can you tell me? I'll let him know, I promise."

"I'd like to talk to both of you if you're free to come over."

"Already gathering Alex's things. I'll pick him up on the way." Dylan put the phone down.

Lily muttered, "What? Seriously! They always make problems out of nothing without listening. But on the other hand, it shows how much they love me."

Almost an hour later, the guys were standing in the ward. Dylan wasn't joking about picking up her brother on the way—he was holding a bag from the store. Lily lay in bed as they sat on the edge of it, opposite each other, so they could both see her well. Their eyes said it all: 'Well, tell us, we're ready to listen.'

"I like a guy." She paused, watching their reactions. "It's not Dan, and most likely, the feeling is mutual."

The guys exchanged glances that Lily couldn't quite decipher before looking back at her.

"Well, that's basically it."

"Lily, if that were all, you wouldn't have called us, would you?"

"I'm scared."

"Of him?"

"No, of the relationship." She began to crumple the bedsheet.

"Has he done something to you?" Dylan asked.

"No, no. I'm just overall afraid of starting a new relationship."

"Because of Dan?" Alex asked. Dylan's stare could burn a hole in his cheek, and Lily just nodded slightly.

"I'm afraid to trust someone again. Do you know how it feels to be an open book that's been soaked with water and then squeezed so that everything is ruined? I don't want to go through that again."

"I understand you, darling, but how can you know what these relationships will be like if you don't try?"

"I still feel like that squeezed book, you know? He helped me dry the pages, and I just started to flatten them back, but as soon as I thought of Dan, I felt crumpled again."

"You want to tell me who he is?"

Lily looked at her brother, then at Dylan, and answered a little hesitantly, "My doctor."

"Benjamin?"

"Uh-huh." She nodded shyly.

"I knew it—I mean, we knew it. Why do we always place the same bets, Dylan? You're no fun to bet with!"

"Because our thoughts constantly overlap." Dylan winked at Alex, who turned up his nose and looked at Lily.

"Benjamin, well, we talked to him recently, and in *our* opinion, we think he realized his feelings for you a little sooner than you did."

Lily blushed, her cheeks turning pink. "Really?"

"Yeah, and if you were talking about him earlier," Dylan added, "I guess you don't have to worry about whether he's serious. He is. And just in case, we've already warned him."

"Warned him about what?" she asked, confused.

"That I shouldn't hurt you," Benjamin said, walking into the room and closing the door behind him. All eyes were on him, each with a different expression. "The door was open." He cleared his throat, pretending he hadn't heard the last few sentences as he came closer, smiling.

"Hi." Lily managed to squeeze out, immediately looking away.

"Hi," he replied, just as embarrassed, knowing what was coming next.

"So, Benjamin, our last conversation in your office wasn't in vain?" Alex asked, with Dylan smiling slightly.

"So, it's true, they were in your office?" Lily asked, startled.

"Yes." Benjamin smiled, walking over to her.

"Why didn't you tell me then?"

"Oh, we had a long conversation about"—Dylan looked at Benjamin in surprise, and his smile grew more pronounced—"that I should be careful with you in every sense of the word, and it ended with the conclusion that I'm a doctor and I know what I'm doing," Benjamin said.

Lily's cheeks flushed deeper, and her eyes began to dart around the room, desperately seeking a place to hide them, just so she wouldn't have to look at the three of them. *Were they seriously discussing this?*

"He's right. We went over everything from safety to the potential for parenthood, and to our surprise, he passed with flying colors on the first try." Alex nodded enthusiastically.

"That's good to hear, Alex," Benjamin said, smiling politely at him, and then sat down on the edge of Lily's bed. "And they also gave us their blessing to start our relationship, and… maybe I'm rushing things, or maybe I'm late, but I want to ask you officially." He cleared his throat and continued, "Will you go out with me?"

Her eyes wandered around the room as she felt a wave of heat and cold pass over her. When Benjamin said those last words, all she wanted to do was cover her eyes with her hands so they wouldn't see the flood of emotions his simple question had unleashed. But before she could lift her hand to her face, Benjamin gently intercepted it, holding it in his and softly stroking the back of her hand with his thumb. Her brother, Dylan, and Benjamin all looked at her, waiting for an answer.

"Alex, Dylan, can you two step outside for a few minutes?" she asked.

The guys exchanged glances.

"Will everything be okay?" Alex asked, and Lily nodded in response.

She waited until they were out of the room, then looked at Benjamin. It was obvious that he was nervous. Her hand was still in his, but his gaze was steady, showing he knew what he wanted.

"You know, it's all so strange and fast. Just now, I had this flash of a memory of that time I got hair on my lips, and honestly, you really annoyed me then. I was scared by the whole situation with Enith, I admit it. And to be honest, I'm afraid to imagine what might happen if we start dating. But I absolutely love our evening talks about the book and its writing, how you fed me, and how you're still trying to, even though it's not necessary now. But that doesn't matter." She went quiet, her gaze dropping to the patterns on the blanket. "You know, I liked you at first sight, but at first, it was just the kind of sympathy that everyone has. Then I got to know you better, and somehow, it started to grow…"

"So that's a 'yes'?" he asked softly.

She looked at him with a light, tender expression, then nodded slightly, confirming her gesture with a smile. Benjamin moved closer and pulled her into a warm, strong bear hug—the kind of hug you give to the most precious treasure, the most fragile gem.

Chapter 23

It was the warmest and most pleasant hug. His arms gently wrapped around my back, and I could feel his heart beating, matching the rhythm of mine. He looked at me with such sincerity, as if to say I could understand everything he wanted to express without words. And in that moment, I knew the feeling was mutual… Meanwhile, my brother and Dylan never returned.

***

I was lying on the bed with a bitter taste in my mouth, realizing that this was my last day in the hospital. Two weeks ago, if someone had offered me the chance to recover at home, I probably would have packed my things, thrown a small backpack on my back, and been out the door in about fifteen minutes—or maybe even faster. Now, the thought of leaving makes my stomach tingle.

Alex promised to pick me up tomorrow. When I suggested alternatives like a taxi or having my girlfriends pick me up, he just looked at me with a stern yet gentle expression. I know he's worried, but I'm worried about him too. Tomorrow, his team has a crucial game that will determine who makes it to the finals and who gets left behind. I know how much he cares about those kids. I've become friends with many of them, and I think they really deserve to make it to the final. Most likely, Alex will have his last training session before the game, which means he's busy. I didn't want to distract him, but the conversation ended where it started, showing his stubbornness and love for me.

Isabel, Olivia, and Emma also volunteered to help me pack and were thrilled to hear I was leaving the hospital. It seemed like everyone was happy except me. They had been trying to convince my brother to let me stay in the dorm again, but he was steadfast almost to the end. Dylan used some of his charms, and my brother eventually softened. I certainly don't mind staying with them, and I know I'll be treated like a princess in a tower guarded by an army of knights.

God, I'm going to cry. This is the last day I'll be able to sit like this with Benjamin and talk or write the book, which, by the way, we still haven't finished.

When he came into my ward as usual at six o'clock and sat down on the edge of the bed next to me, I held my breath. How handsome he looked. I stared at him, hoping to memorize every new wrinkle, every birthmark that adorned his appearance, especially the two that were paired next to his left eye. His stubborn hair was as pleasant to the touch as it seemed. And the lips… oh my God, I got carried away…

***

"Lily, love, you're staring. Do you see something interesting?" he asked boldly, barely holding back a smile.

"Yeah, I'm trying to memorize all the curves and lines of this beautiful sculpture," she answered freely, continuing where she left off.

"Is it really that beautiful?" He raised an eyebrow.

"Believe me, even you won't be able to appreciate it properly," she replied, raising her eyebrows.

"It's strange. I've been living with it for a long time. Why do you say that?"

"You're not a woman, that's why. We know better." She hummed, holding out her hands to him.

"I agree, that's an interesting statement." A smile spread across his face as he dove into her arms.

"I'm going to miss… these evenings."

"I know, dear, I know. Me too. But we're not saying goodbye forever." He pulled away slightly to look into the ocean of her eyes.

"It's not forever, but it's still hard. I have college; you have work… it's just hard."

"Yeah, doesn't that remind you of the characters in your book?"

"It's not funny! At least they're in the same college!" She puffed out her cheeks, and Benjamin pulled her into a hug again.

"Okay, bad joke. I'll miss you too. But honey, like it or not, I'm going to jump over your brother in your contact list. Do you mind?" He playfully raised both eyebrows.

"Try it. Alex writes to me a lot, especially recently," she said.

"Then I'll write even more."

"We'll see."

For a while, they were just silent, as if they could understand each other without words.

"We will finish the book, won't we?"

"Of course."

"Are you sure you'll have time for that?"

"Lily, darling, are you seriously doubting whether I'll have time for you?"

"I'm sorry. I know you will."

He kissed her gently on the cheek. "How do you plan to celebrate Christmas?"

"I don't know yet. Maybe this year, I'll keep up the tradition of watching *The Grinch* with a plate of turkey and cranberry juice on my lap in a room decorated with Christmas lights." He proudly finished describing his tradition, and Lily laughed.

"That's cute."

"Do you really think so?"

"Of course. I love *The Grinch,* turkey, and lights." She added silently with a look, *And you.*

"Is it just me, or is my girlfriend a real angel?" he said theatrically.

"Come on; you're imagining things." Lily winked.

That evening, for the first time, they couldn't tear themselves away from the conversation long enough to write anything for the book.

Chapter 24

That morning didn't start with the usual: "Good morning, how did you sleep?" but instead with an enthusiastic, "God, I'm so glad you're coming back to the dormitory!" If only I could borrow a bit of her joy, because according to the nurse, my face was so sour, it looked like I'd eaten an entire lemon. My brother arrived in the afternoon with Dylan, and they told the girls to wait for me at the dorm. I barely had time to say goodbye to Benjamin; he was called away to some emergency after just five minutes, and then I was on my way home.

Now I'm back, surrounded by familiar walls, a bed with a dip in the middle of the mattress, and a light cobweb in the corner of the room—everything's the same as before. I unpacked the few things I had, only to realize the girls were nowhere to be found. The bathroom was empty, and the kitchen was unusually quiet. I wandered out into the corridor, wondering if they'd gone to see a neighbor, but just then, I saw them cheerfully making their way toward our room.

"Lily, are you home already?" Olivia asked, sounding confused.

"Better rephrase that; it sounds like you're not happy to see me."

"All right, all right, but how long have you been here?" Isabel chimed in.

"About ten minutes ago. Why?"

"I told you to hurry, and you were like, 'No, everything will be fine. Don't worry, we'll be on time.' And then, 'Look at this sale! How can we miss it?'" Olivia shot a squinty-eyed glare at Emma.

"Okay, my bad, but the sale was really good, right?" Emma defended herself.

"But the surprise is ruined!" Olivia huffed.

"Then why not just throw a party?"

"Everything's so simple with you! And where are the gifts? Where's the unexpected reaction?"

"Girls, sorry to interrupt, but what's the surprise?" I asked, trying to keep up with the conversation.

"It's all her fault," Olivia snapped, pointing at Emma. "It's because of her!"

"Come on, I didn't mean to ruin anything!"

"Forget them. We're having a party tonight. Have you eaten yet?" Isabel interjected, giving me a friendly hug. "I bought your favorite pizza."

"Cheese?"

"Yup."

I beamed, and we headed into the room, leaving the other two to their bickering.

"Wait, but I can't eat pizza," I said, suddenly remembering. I paused before adding, "Just one slice."

"I'm not offering you more than that." Isabel laughed, placing a slice on a plate.

Within moments, Olivia and Emma joined us, clearly having settled their quarrel, though neither wore a victorious expression.

"Can you two sit quietly in the kitchen for ten minutes, or better yet, fifteen?" Olivia asked, glaring at Emma.

"Yeah, we really need it," said Emma, only to get a pinch and wordless 'need?' from Olivia.

"I mean, we want to catch our breath and change. Do you mind?" Emma corrected herself.

"It's fine. We were planning to stay a while anyway," I reassured them, glancing at Isabel.

She nodded in agreement.

For the next fifteen minutes, various sounds—from joyful laughter to cracks and screams, emanated from the room. Finally, both friends reappeared in the kitchen. "Lily, would you join us in the room?"

I furrowed my brows, sensing what was coming. As soon as I crossed the threshold, the girls set off party poppers from both sides. While I laughed and picked confetti out of my hair, my eyes caught sight of a table near the TV. It was surrounded by balloons, and the table itself was covered with popcorn and other snacks. The TV was playing a movie we'd been wanting to watch together for a long time. It seemed like a small gesture, but it was so heartwarming. I didn't even notice the smile spreading across my face, but it was the signal my friends had been waiting for. In an instant, they were hugging me and shouting, "Welcome back!"

***

The movie lasted almost three hours, so we took a break after the first hour. Emma and Isabel went to the kitchen to get some fresh water, while Olivia headed to the bathroom. I stayed on the couch in front of the TV, flipping through my phone messages. Nothing new. The old ones had long been deleted. I was surprised to see that Benjamin had messaged me almost immediately after I left the hospital. Well, not immediately, by then I was nearly at the dorm, but still. He asked how I got home and if I made it back safely. It was kind of corny but also sweet.

A phone beside me started vibrating continuously, catching my attention. I glanced over to see whose it was, noticing notifications popping up one after the other on the screen:

"You said you would deal with…"

"Wasn't the fucking toilet enough? Why didn't that stop her then?"

"Listen, if this comes out, we have nothing to do with it."

"We were only following your instructions! It doesn't matter that you're the head of the fan club! I'm done. You can throw water on me or lock me up too! I don't care! I want nothing to do with this. She ended up in the hospital because of him. Isn't that enough for you?"

I blinked, struggling to make sense of what I was seeing. The phone belonged to Emma. Emma is my friend; she couldn't possibly be the head of the club that bullied me… but even if she was, what did it mean? I had no idea what was going on in her head. Maybe she just didn't like me for some reason. Or maybe I was misunderstanding everything.

Isabel returned to the room, and I tried to calm down. When Emma came back, her phone was exactly where she'd left it. I know I shouldn't have touched it, but if I hadn't, I'd still be in the dark. It's a double-edged sword.

"Emma, can I ask you a quick question?" I tried to put on a smile.

"Sure."

"What do you know about Dan's fan club?"

Olivia approached just as I was finishing my question, and the girls perked up their ears.

Emma gulped noticeably and replied, "Not much, just a bunch of girls who are crazy about Dan."

"And what is it about him that's so crazy?" I pressed further.

"Who knows? Every girl has her own interests," she said shrugging, trying to appear calm.

"And what's the purpose of it?" I raised an eyebrow in interest.

"To keep other girls from getting too close to Dan." She bit her lip nervously.

"And who created it?"

"How should I know?"

"Then let's ask Lin or whatever her name is. She just wrote to you, saying she was done with your games and wasn't going to act on your behalf anymore," I said, keeping my voice steady.

Emma swallowed hard, her eyes locked on mine as she responded in a nervous voice, "Why the fuck were you going through my phone?"

"No, the real question is, why are you doing this behind my back?"

"It started before you two even met!"

As the saying goes, 'When you tell people your secrets, you put a knife in their hands.'

"What are you talking about?" Olivia asked, confused.

"She's the head of Dan's fan club and the mastermind behind everything that happened to me," I said, shaking my head in Emma's direction. I didn't want any scandals; I didn't see the point.

"Is it true?" Isabel asked, her voice tense.

"Yes, it's true! It's true! What else do you want to hear?" Emma snapped. "She's been pissing me off this whole time—a gray mouse thinking she can jump over her own head. Do you think you were worth it? You're wrong, so wrong. He found a replacement for you quickly enough. As for the gossip and all that, it was too easy to organize. In college, you only need to know a few people to spread rumors, and there goes the magic." She paused, considering what more to say.

Isabel asked calmly, "Do you need help packing?"

"What?" Emma asked in shock.

"I said, do you want to pack your own clothes, or do you need help?"

"What the hell are you talking about?" Emma's voice rose in disbelief.

"Emma, you're not living here anymore. I'll arrange with the residence hall director to find you a new place. You're not staying here."

"And why is that?" Emma crossed her arms defiantly.

"At least because no one wants to see you, let alone talk to you. Get up, Emma." Isabel started throwing Emma's belongings into her suitcase.

Maybe she felt sorry, maybe not—but she didn't show it, didn't apologize. Emma just walked out with all her things and slammed the door behind her.

I sat on the couch, watching the events unfold in the room, my eyes shifting from one friend to another. Tears welled up, but I fought to hold them back. A whirlwind of emotions swept over me, from seething anger to a deep sense of pity. I was furious that my friend had lied to me, staging all those attempts to humiliate me in public. But at the same time, I felt a pang of sorrow, knowing I was losing a friend like this.

As I mentioned earlier, you often hand people a knife without even knowing what kind of person they are or what to expect from them. It's one of the cruelest realities of life because the closest person can carry that knife for years before striking, and you might even forget it exists.

The girls went to the bedroom, leaving me alone with my thoughts. My vision blurred. I found my phone and, with trembling fingers, dialed Benjamin's number. I knew he was at work, probably busy, but I desperately needed to hear his voice.

"Hi, honey, how are you?"

"I wanted to hear your voice, so I called."

"That's cruel, so you missed the voice not the conversations?"

"I missed them, too." I smiled, even though I knew he couldn't see it.

"I'm glad to hear that. So, how's home?"

"Everything's great—well, maybe not everything, but right now I'm the happiest."

"Because you love me?"

"Yeah. You're not busy, by the way? I'm not distracting you from work?"

"No, not at all. I'm just sitting in my office, sorting out documents."

"I'm not bothering you?"

"Not at all. By the way, have you eaten anything yet?"

"Yes, but I'm embarrassed to say… I know you won't praise me… but that slice of cheese pizza was too tasty to resist. It must have been magnetic; I couldn't take my eyes off it."

"Well, I certainly won't praise you for eating junk food, but I will praise you for sticking to just one slice. You're doing great with your willpower. How are you feeling after it?"

"I'm fine, don't worry."

"I'm going to worry anyway; the mother of my children should be healthy." He laughed, and I almost choked on my water.

"W-what?"

"I love you too," he teased.

"I like your voice; it calms me down."

"Do you want me to record a voice message for you? You can listen to it when I can't talk."

"Sure." I smiled again, feeling the joy in his voice.

"Okay, what would you like? A bedtime story, maybe? *Cinderella* or *Sleeping Beauty*?"

"Let's go with *Cinderella*."

"All right, then tonight we're going to travel through the castle."

That day, I fell asleep just before the beautiful coach turned back into a pumpkin.

***

When I returned to college, I was surprised to see that the blatant bullying had stopped. No one was whispering about me anymore, and I was relieved. But there was one uncomfortable change—they didn't say anything about me or to me at all. At first, it made me angry, but then I realized it wasn't worth wasting my time and energy on them.

Christmas was approaching, and as I mentioned earlier, I just love it. Even though I didn't have much time, I still managed to find gifts. For my brother and Dylan, I chose two nearly identical sets: a box of Christmas cookies paired with warm, Christmas-themed socks. For the girls, it was easy to pick out toys and sweets—who could resist a gingerbread Christmas tree or a little gingerbread snowman during the holidays?

My last gift, though, was really hard to choose. I spent about three hours wandering through the shop rows, which had been decorated with Christmas lights and cute toys for weeks. It wasn't just about creating an atmosphere; it was pure marketing because, when you're looking for a themed gift, you can't help but be drawn in. I ended up visiting thirteen stores, and do you think I found what I needed? Not even close! I left each one empty-handed, moving from one shop to the next.

Just as I was distracted by the beautiful lights outside the window of the next shop, my phone vibrated. It was a message from Benjamin.

"Hi, whatcha doing?"

"Still hunting for Christmas gifts. How about you?"

"Been at home for a while now. Any luck?"

"It's not as easy as I thought, but I'm getting there. It's hard to find one last gift."

"I see. So, does this mean you won't be able to spend Christmas with me? I have the day off, and I don't really have any plans."

"I'm sorry, I haven't talked to my brother about it yet."

"I get it. Well, as they say, 'Hope dies last,' right?"

"Well, someone's in a positive mood."

"I try. Are you cold?"

"Now that you mention it, I didn't notice how close my fingers were to turning into icicles."

"Wow, you must be really focused."

"You bet! Did you think picking out the perfect gift would be easy?"

"I'm afraid to even imagine. Now I understand why I've never quite hit the mark with gifts. I guess I never paid them much attention."

"You see, that's a big mistake."

"Yeah, I'll remember that."

"Are you laughing over there?"

"What makes you think that? I just enjoy hearing your life lessons."

"Glad to hear it. Have you finished picking out your gifts?"

"A while ago."

"You're full of surprises. Honestly, I'm dreaming of curling up on the couch with a blanket and a cup of tea. I'm trying to warm up with the thought of it, and it's actually working. The trick is to imagine it all in detail."

"You see, I'm just trying to turn all your thoughts into reality. But are you really going to give up on spending Christmas together? Don't break my heart, love."

"Smooth talker. What's next? Are you going to tell me you're wearing a warm knitted Christmas sweater?"

"Well, actually, I am. How did you know? Wait, did you leave a camera in my apartment? Is it just in this room, or are there more?"

"If I had, I would've come up with something more original."

"Too bad. But seriously, why did you ask? Wait! Don't tell me you're wearing something thin."

"I didn't plan on being out this late."

"So, what are you wearing?"

"A dress."

"And that's it? What about warm tights? A hat and scarf?"

"My tights aren't very warm, but I've got a hat and scarf. I'm fine."

"Where did you say you were shopping?"

"In the center, near the cinema. I've been browsing the shops with Christmas displays. I'm almost at the end of the street."

"Okay, go into the nearest store. I'll be there in five minutes."

"Wait, why?"

"To take you home."

That's when it hit me—why not get him something he'll actually use? I skipped the next store and went straight to a men's clothing shop. After a bit of searching, I found exactly what I was looking for: a warm, patterned knitted sweater that seemed to be waiting just for me. I quickly picked it up and rushed to the checkout, hoping to pay before my boyfriend arrived and saw his unwrapped gift.

Chapter 25

Benjamin arrived quickly, just as he'd promised. I still felt a bit shy about how close we'd become. Not too long ago, he was just the doctor who kept an eye on my diet and treated my burn. Now, he's opening the passenger door of his car for me like a true gentleman, motioning for me to get in. I slid into the seat with a smile.

He circled around to the driver's side, started the engine, and sat in silence, deep in thought. I gently slid my hand over to his, and without taking his eyes off the road, he covered my hand with his own. I let out a quiet sigh of relief as he began to softly rub my palm with his thumb, trying to warm me.

"I should have picked you up sooner; you're freezing," he said, his lips pressed in concern. It was clear he was worried about more than just the cold.

"I'm warm now, and I wasn't outside for long. Honestly, it was way too hot in the stores," I reassured him, rubbing his hand. His shoulders relaxed slightly.

"Are you sure?" he asked.

"Yeah," I replied, leaning over to kiss him on the cheek.

"So, how did your shopping go? Did you find gifts for everyone?" He smiled, and as always, it took my breath away.

"Yes, I did. Everyone's covered," I chirped.

"And you got something for me too?" he teased.

"Of course! You didn't think I'd leave you without a gift, did you? Don't worry, even if it's something as simple as socks, I'm sure you'd be happy to wear them to work every day. So, be prepared!" I said with a playful grin.

"Are you suggesting I wear the same pair every day?" he joked.

"Well, not exactly. I'd give you a big pack—you could go two weeks before washing them all."

"Please tell me you didn't buy me socks," he pleaded, and I couldn't help but smile.

"Who knows? Who knows?" I teased.

"All right, all right," he said with mock resignation.

"You know, it's not such a bad idea. I could save water by washing them all in bulk. Thanks for the inspiration."

"For what?" he asked.

"For the idea of a future gift." I winked at him playfully, and he let out a dramatic sigh.

"So, no socks for me?" he asked with a pout.

"Sorry, no socks this time."

"Such a pity. I had so many plans for them," he said, giving me the cutest, most pitiful look, like Puss in Boots from *Shrek*.

"Ever thought about applying to drama school?" I joked.

"I tried, but they turned me down. They actually said, 'Your level is too high for our institution. Try somewhere else; good luck!' Can you believe that?"

"I can," I said laughing. "And then you decided being a doctor was that higher level?"

"Exactly! I think they only accepted me because of my grandiose performance. I had to pass an oral exam with all the boring medical terminology, just like everyone else, but I added a little flair to it. Not everyone got it, but those who did appreciated it. And that's how I landed a scholarship and ended up here."

We reached the dorm, and Benjamin turned off the engine. I found myself torn between the urge to stay with him and the need to go upstairs for some warm tea to avoid getting sick. It was already completely dark outside, with snowflakes gently falling from the sky, covering everything in a soft, magical white dust—like something out of a fairy tale.

I clasped my hands on my knees and looked over at Benjamin. "Thank you for coming to get me."

"It's nothing, really," he replied with a wink, starting to turn toward the door, but I stopped him.

"Lily?"

"I don't want to go," I said, running my hand over his cheek, searching his eyes for the same reluctance.

"I know, love; I don't want you to go either, but you need to. I don't want your brother to worry, and I promised him I'd protect you like a precious gem," he said, leaning his forehead against mine.

"You did? Didn't you promise something else?" I teased with a playful smile.

"That too," he murmured before intercepting my words with a kiss. His fingers gently combed through my hair, and the kiss was soft, almost weightless.

When he pulled away, I felt a pang of sadness. I sat there for a few more seconds, watching as Benjamin walked around to the backseat to grab the packages. I quickly jumped out to retrieve my last purchase first.

"Need help carrying them?" he asked, juggling what looked like half the store in his hands—pink bags stuffed full, and a box tucked under his arm. The sight of him standing there, arms full of Christmas shopping, brought back memories of the Panthers teasing me with remarks like: "Isn't it time you got a boyfriend?" or "Don't you have someone to help you with all those heavy bags?" I used to brush those comments off, but now, seeing Benjamin like this, I realized how wrong I was—this was an incredible sight.

"Of course, I'd be very grateful," I said, and we began walking up the stairs together—me with my package, his gift, and him with the rest. He walked ahead of me, giving me a view of his broad, muscular back that I loved so much. It radiated protection and safety, along with that comforting scent of Benjamin.

Given my lingering panic about relationships, which I had discussed with my brother and later with Benjamin, we agreed to take things slow, avoiding any big steps. He assured me that he was willing to wait as long as I needed, and I felt confident in his words. I appreciated how gentle he was and how much he valued my opinion, especially when it came to our relationship. But sometimes, I caught myself wondering. *Could he really be satisfied with where we are now? I feel like a walking problem, a child who's never been in a normal relationship. Maybe he wants a family, children, or something more. What can I give him right now?*

"Earth to Lily, hello?" His warm hand on my cold cheek brought me back to reality.

"Yes?" I replied, all my doubts fading when I saw his eyes.

"Will you open the door? It's cold in the stairwell."

"Oh, of course," I mumbled, fumbling to unlock the door, clearly flustered.

"Can I come in?"

"The girls aren't back yet, so we won't disturb anyone," I said, quickly stashing his gift in my closet and placing the rest of the packages on my bed.

"Tea or coffee?"

"Tea, please. No sugar."

"Got it," I said, turning on the kettle and pulling out my entire stash of teas. "Take your pick."

"Wow, that's quite the collection. It's hard to choose!"

"Take your time; the water hasn't boiled yet," I said smiling, sitting down across from him.

"This one," he finally decided.

"Great choice. I love that one too; you've got good taste."

"I've got a good teacher." He flashed me one of his most charming smiles, and I nearly spilled the boiling water on my fingers.

We spent the next while talking—about my childhood, Alex, the Panthers, the book we were almost finished with, his family, and so much more…

Chapter 26

Actually, I'm not spending Christmas with my brother this year. We talked about it as soon as I got out of the hospital. While my brother was initially reluctant, Dylan was completely supportive, and eventually, my brother came around too.

I gave the girls their gifts two days before Christmas since we're all heading home for the holidays and wouldn't be able to exchange them later. They surprised me with a few gifts as well: socks with Christmas trees, homemade cookies, some cute trinkets, and lots of good vibes. Honestly, even if they'd only given me a single candy, I'd still be just as happy—I adore these girls.

Tomorrow morning, I'll drop off gifts for my brother and Dylan before they head out of town to celebrate with all the Panthers. I'm just hoping public transportation runs on Christmas Day.

As for Benjamin, I spent the entire day running around my room, trying on different dresses, jewelry, and shoes. I want to surprise him, to make him feel special. I imagine him opening the door, not expecting anyone, and then—ta-dah! I know it sounds easier than it really is, and it's probably not the most well-thought-out plan, but it doesn't matter. The main thing is that I'll be with him. I settled on a black silk dress with a slit on the right leg and a pair of black heels. A warm fur coat over the top, and I'm ready to go conquer his already conquered heart.

It might sound childish, but I made the cards for each gift by hand, painting and decorating them with imaginary Christmas socks, putting a piece of my soul into each one. I stayed up late finishing Benjamin's card, and at some point, I worried I was overdoing it. But is that really such a bad thing? The brighter, the better, right? Anyway, I went to bed way too late.

The next morning, I deeply regretted skipping P.E. classes in school. I didn't hear the alarm clock until almost an hour after it first started ringing. I had to cosplay one of my favorite TV shows from childhood, nothing funny about that! If I couldn't remember anything from school, I could at least try to fly like a Winx fairy, hoping it would speed up my movements.

Dressed in my planned outfit, I glanced at my watch. Ten minutes until the bus was supposed to arrive—if it showed up at all. There wasn't any time for makeup, so I looked in the mirror, muttered something like, "Fairies don't wear makeup, they're beautiful as they are," and dashed out to the bus stop.

Luckily, Alex and Dylan were still at home when I arrived. The day flew by in a blur of great company, delicious food, and lots of fun, but even that couldn't distract me from my plans for the evening. I knew Benjamin was planning to celebrate Christmas at home, so I didn't even ask if he'd be there, though maybe I should have.

At five o'clock, I suddenly jumped to my feet as if I'd been electrocuted, and headed out to meet my adventure—or, more accurately, to see my boyfriend. It was quite cold outside, and for a moment, I regretted my choice of clothes, but the thought that it would all be worth it kept me going. My anxiety only grew as I reached the entrance to his building. I wasn't scared of him but of the situation itself. *Could something go wrong? Why am I even thinking about that?* I shook off those thoughts—they were as welcome as a third wheel right now—and slowly climbed the long stairs to the third floor. Each step felt like an eternity.

At his door, I took a deep breath, then another. I reset my brain, hoping it would prove useful, and pressed the doorbell. I didn't let go for a few seconds, and when my thoughts finally caught up to the present, I heard something crash behind the door, followed by a muffled voice. Then, the key turned, and the door opened. I dared to look up. God, he was so beautiful with his messy hair and casual home clothes. I almost drooled but managed to pull myself together.

"Hi, you look fantastic," I greeted Benjamin.

"Hello, thank you! I didn't expect to see you here. Come in," he replied, visibly confused.

"You didn't? If you knew how long I've been dreaming about today… It's good that you're home."

"I thought I said I didn't have any plans," he responded, still a bit puzzled as he led me to the kitchen. "Would you like a warm drink? You must be freezing."

"Sure, so now it's your turn to treat me with tea and candies?"

"Well, I have cake too," he said with a cheeky smile, and I couldn't resist.

"Seriously? And you kept quiet about that this whole time? Bring it out, bring it out—we'll finish it in no time!"

"Aren't you afraid that cake, tea, and candy on top might not be good for you?" he asked with an innocent look.

"Are you afraid that if I gain a few extra pounds, you'll fall out of love with me?" I teased, feigning surprise.

"No, my girl will be beautiful no matter what."

"I knew you'd say that! So, I guess you don't mind if I take three slices and leave you two?"

"Of course not."

"Oh wait, I have something for you. I want you to see it now," I said, rummaging through my nearly bottomless bag until I finally pulled out his gift. "I hope you like it."

"Hmm, I hope so too," he replied, and I playfully pinched his arm.

"So, he hopes, huh?"

"I'm just kidding, honey. Whatever it is, I'm sure it's beautiful. Give me a minute; I'll go get the scissors."

"You can take it with you and open it there," I called after him.

"Okay!"

I took a sip of tea, then another with a piece of candy. When he returned, he was wearing the sweater I'd given him—it looked like it was made for him!

"It looks great on you!"

"Thank you, it's very comfy and warm," he said, coming over to gently kiss my cheek. "I have something for you too," he added, handing me a small, well-wrapped box.

I began to open it carefully, while Benjamin watched me in his new sweater. Beneath the Christmas wrapping was a box filled with packaging paper. Digging a little deeper, I felt the top of a small ball. When I pulled it out, my eyes sparkled. It was a beautiful glass Christmas ornament. Inside was a decorated Christmas tree, children gathered around it, and Santa flying in his sleigh overhead, all surrounded by falling snow that shifted with every movement. For a moment, I felt tears sting my eyes—I loved Benjamin's gift more than I could express. You bet I liked it! I'd been dreaming about a glass Christmas ball since I was a little girl, but back then there were more problems than glass balls. And later I had to put aside my childhood dreams.

I pulled him into a big hug. "Did you know this was my childhood dream?" I whispered into his chest.

"No, I didn't, but I had a feeling you'd like it," he replied gently, holding me close.

"And you were right," I said, thanking him with a gentle kiss on the cheek. "By the way, what are our plans for the evening?" I asked, pulling back slightly to look into his eyes.

"To eat sweets with tea…"

"Well, that's obvious, but then what?"

"Let's watch a movie," he suggested, handing me another candy.

"Good idea! Let's watch *The Grinch*," I begged, and he exhaled in mock defeat.

"Sure, and after that, *Home Alone*?"

"Okay! Shall we start with the first one?"

"Of course, the first two are classics."

"I agree," I said, popping the candy into my mouth with a satisfied smile.

The evening was perfect: *The Grinch*, cake with tea, *Home Alone*, more candies, *Home Alone 2*, another piece of cake, lots of hugs, *Home Alone 3*, even more hugs, and a gentle kiss. The night was long, magical, and filled with wonderful emotions and warmth from the one I loved.

Epilogue

Lily

I made myself a strong berry tea and settled on the sofa by the window. It was already lunchtime, and the beautiful weather outside charged me with a positive mood. I pulled my laptop onto my lap and opened the document I had been working on for the past six months. In a moment, words began to appear on the screen as fast as if they were being spoken instead of written.

This is my third book. I still can't believe that Benjamin convinced me to send my first book, *The Game*, to a publisher, and that three out of twenty people were actually interested in it. Now, I have my own audience waiting for my books, and what could be better for an author than that?

A slight rustle from the baby monitor distracted me from my writing. I quietly went to the next room—everything was fine, Melissa was still sleeping. I often sit by my daughter's bedside, marveling at how small and adorable she is, and how much she looks like Benjamin. Alex says she got her eyebrows and lips from me, while Dylan mentions something about her nose, but honestly, they confuse me. All I see is the spitting image of my husband. They're both beautiful.

As if hearing my thoughts, Melissa smiled in her sleep and turned her face toward me, reaching out with her tiny hand. "You are so beautiful," I whispered. "You should know how many people loved you long before you were born."

Benjamin

Today is a quiet day at work—no scheduled surgeries—but I'm always ready for emergencies. I am sitting in my office, sorting through a mountain of documents that had accumulated over the past few days. On my desk, there's a photo of Lily holding Melissa in her arms. God, am I the luckiest man alive?

The nurse whispers to me to stop smiling for no reason maybe five times a day, saying it looks strange. But she just hasn't seen my princesses. In the photo, they're both dressed in lavender dresses, and Lily is feeding Melissa milk from a bottle painted with lavender. Melissa is an exact copy of Lily, with curly hair and those pretty doll-like eyes... *Okay, Ben, control yourself; others might not really understand.*